THE CURSE OF FLOUR AND FEELING

LOU WILHAM

Midnight Tide
PUBLISHING

Created with Vellum

ALSO BY LOU WILHAM

The Curse Collection
    The Curse of The Black Cat
    The Curse of Ash and Blood
    The Curse of Flour and Feeling

The Sea Witch Trilogy
    Tales of the Sea Witch
    Tales of the Littlest Mermaid

The Clockwork Chronicles
    The Girl in the Clockwork Tower
    The Unicorn and the Clockwork Quest

Villainous Heroics
    Villainous

The Heir To Moondust
    The Prince of Starlight
    The Prince of Daybreak

*To anyone who needs a
little magic in their life.*

THE CURSE OF
ASH & BLOOD
LOU WILHAM

PROLOGUE

Not so long ago—in a city you may or may not be familiar with known as New York—there lived a young girl by the name of Darcie Gyeong Alston. Named so for her dark hair, dark eyes, and her mother's family name, Gyeong. The Gyeongs were bakers, had been bakers for generations in Korea, and Gyeong Eun, in spite of having never known another home outside of New York, was no different. Thus, Darcie was raised, as baker's children so often are, like dough. In a warm kitchen, freckled with flour, and sweetened by sugar. And it was understood, always, that one day she would be a baker herself.

A few short blocks away—a world away by New York standards—there lived a child named Atsushi Haruki, but from a young age, zir friends just called zir Hari. Hari was bright, and charming, and clever. The kind of child who drew everyone into zir orbit. The kind of child who never had trouble making friends. With a creative spirit and a quick mind, ze saw potential everywhere ze looked.

ONE

The sun was shining the day she met them. There was no family there now. Just the cold, unforgiving earth digging into her knees, the smell of snow on the air, and the headstone gleaming in the watery winter light.

And the sun was shining—Darcie remembered that clearly because she wondered why the sun would be shining when she was so sad. Why the sun would dare show its face as she knelt by the grave of her eomma and swallowed back the tears she couldn't let fall when it wasn't raining for fear someone might see.

Eomma had told Darcie not to cry for her just before she had died, sitting in the bed surrounded by machines intent on keeping her alive and failing. She'd said this was but the first of her three lives, and they would meet again. Darcie didn't think she believed in reincarnation, but she hoped eomma was right.

Still, not a week later, they had buried her. The cold earth just barely giving way in the middle of December. It had rained *that* day, and Darcie had been grateful for it.

Had hidden her tears in the soft droplets to keep the rest of the family from seeing.

Darcie reached out to remove the dried bundle of flowers left behind by one of the ajummas from the bakery. It was sweet that they'd come and left flowers for eomma, but it made something twist in her belly. Something she didn't recognize. They had to know that the bakery would be closing soon. They had to know that she couldn't keep it open by herself. She had school to think of. Still, they came and paid their respects.

It was sweet.

She hated it.

The flowers crumbled in her harsh grip. Dried petals catching on the wind and fluttering away to brush against the other gravestones. She'd come to tell eomma that they would have to close the bakery. She'd come to tell her that she was leaving the city, moving somewhere less expensive so she could finish high school and then start college—not that she had even applied anywhere yet. She'd come to say goodbye to eomma and appa. But the words clung like dough without enough flour, sticky and thick in her throat.

She opened her mouth to try to force them out. It would hurt she was sure, but she was ready for that, or she thought she was anyhow. Something glittered out of the corner of her eye, and the words stilled in her throat. Lips pressing together, Darcie glanced over at the person standing a few headstones away. Their dress had sparkles on it. Who wore a sparkly dress to a graveyard?

"It's New Year's," the person said when they caught Darcie glaring at them. "You should look nice on New Year's."

"This is a place of mourning, not a club." Darcie

snapped her eyes back to her eomma's name on the gravestone.

"Point stands." The person's footsteps hadn't crunched on the still frosted-over grass, but suddenly they were standing beside her. Their glittering dress glaring in Darcie's periphery. "What're you doing out this early on New Year's, anyway? You're just a kid. Shouldn't you still be in bed nursing a hang over?"

"Leave me alone." The flowers made a soft rustling sound when Darcie's hands trembled around them. She refused to look down to watch them shake apart, or up to meet the person's searching gaze. She stared straight ahead, watching the reflection of the clouds on eomma's polished headstone.

"My name's Gwydion," they said like they hadn't heard Darcie. She knew they had.

"I don't care."

"You should. You called me here."

"I don't even know who you *are*." Darcie ground her teeth, molars squeaking against each other. Why wasn't she getting up? Why wasn't she just walking away? It would be so easy.

The person—Gwydion—let out a soft sound that sounded like a laugh but was eaten up by the breeze and the quiet of so many dead things. "I'm your fairy dragmother of course!"

Darcie's head whipped around, staring up at Gwydion through narrowed eyes. "Excuse me?"

"I think you heard me just fine." Gwydion knelt down beside Darcie, likely soiling their impossibly expensive dress. "You called me here because you have a wish you want to make."

"No. I don't." Darcie jerked her head back to the gravestone, ignoring the way her dark hair brushed into her eyes. She needed a haircut. Eomma had said as much three weeks ago, but there hadn't been time. Now . . . now she supposed it didn't matter; no one would see her hair that mattered.

"You do. Everyone who seeks me out does."

"I didn't seek you out. I just came here to tell eomma that . . . to tell her that . . . " Darcie bit down hard on the inside of her cheek. There would be a sore there in a few hours, but just like her hair, it didn't matter.

"Do you really not have anything you want?" Gwydion's voice had gone quiet, lost much of its exuberance, as if they were afraid of scaring Darcie off.

"I just want . . . " Her eyes were blurry with tears. She sniffed, scrubbing them away with the back of her sleeve. "I want eomma's bakery to succeed."

"Is that your wish?"

"Yes," she said, eighteen and not even really sure what she was asking for. But she knew it was the truth. That right in that moment, that's all she wanted, to see eomma's bakery thrive as it once had when she'd been too young to work the stand mixer.

"And you're sure? That's kind of a—You know what? No. You're right. I did make a resolution to give everyone exactly what they asked for. So I'll give you this." Gwydion's earrings jingled as they nodded to themselves.

Darcie blinked back more tears, breathing through the tightness in her chest. It was becoming harder to focus through the pounding of her heart in her ears. The characters on eomma and appa's gravestones swam in front of her eyes.

Something sparkled brightly at the corner of her vision. Gwydion's obnoxiously lovely dress, she was sure. She didn't turn to look at them. She couldn't. Not until she got control over herself. Not until she wrestled the tears back to where they belonged.

"I hope it makes you happy," Gwydion said so softly that Darcie almost didn't hear it. And then they were gone. They didn't walk away. They simply . . . disappeared. There wasn't even an indent where they'd knelt in the grass beside her.

"Weird." Darcie shook her head and put it from her mind. There were other things to worry about.

IT HAD BEEN years since Darcie had thought of them. The tall slim figure standing out like a beacon amongst the graves, with their red tresses and shimmering midnight-blue grown dragging through the crunching grass. The one who said they would grant her wish. The one who'd disappeared like the frost a few hours after sunrise, with no sign that they'd been there at all.

Her "fairy dragmother".

Gwydion.

So long, in fact, that Darcie had convinced herself it had been a dream. She'd been grieving. She'd been stressed. She didn't know what to do at the time. She was eighteen and she'd just been orphaned. She was going to lose the bakery. She was going to have to move away from the only home she'd ever known. Of course she had conjured up some glittering savior. Some beautiful creature who would make everything all better.

And after that . . . after she'd left the cemetery and returned to the bakery to prepare the buns for the day, Gwydion had quickly faded from her mind. There was too much else to do in the days that followed. Especially when the ajammas from the bakery banded together and demanded that Darcie stay, offering her a room at one of their apartments so she didn't have to leave the city. They'd even helped with the books and the management of Gyeong's while Darcie finished her diploma and took classes online.

The first couple of years had been tough; they had been a lot of hard work. But Darcie had been happy. She had watched eomma's dream flourish in ways she'd never thought possible. And so long as Darcie had her nose buried in her studies and her arms elbow-deep in dough, she didn't really notice anything else.

Then the ajammas had begun to retire. The neighborhood changed. Gyeong's, which had once been a small local spot, had become a tourist attraction.

But now . . . now that red head of curls was standing in the middle of the mayhem of the Saturday morning rush. Turning this way and that as Gwydion followed the racing of Darcie's staff from the back of the shop to the glass cases in the front window as they tried to prep before they were hit with the early-bird tourists. Maybe Gwydion was just there to get some pastries and then they'd be on their way. It had been six years, after all.

A girl—one of the ten Sarahs that worked at Gyeongs during the summer—yelped, skidding around Gwydion and almost dropping the pan of hot mocha buns to the floor.

"Be careful!" Darcie shouted, her eyes narrowed on Sarah dangerously.

"Sorry! Sorry!" Sarah offered Gwydion a tight smile and continued on her way to the window.

A buzzer rang in the back, signaling a finished bake. Darcie's head jerked to the bored looking twentysomething

—Heather—leaning against the glass case. "Are you going to get that?"

"Sure thing, boss." Heather gave Darcie a lazy salute and went to the back to retrieve whatever it was.

Darcie pulled on her customer-service smile and turned back to Gwydion, who was watching her with a vague look of upset. "Welcome to Gyeong's. What can I get for you today?"

"You don't *look* happy," Gwydion said without missing a beat. She'd hoped Gwydion wouldn't recognize her . . . *No such luck,* Darcie thought, resisting the urge to slouch.

"Excuse me?" Darcie's smile slipped a fraction, only held up by years of practice, and the want to get Gwydion out of the shop as soon as possible so she could focus on other, more important things.

"You said success would make you happy." Gwydion's expression had gone from upset to truly troubled. "I only granted your wish because I thought it'd make you happy."

"Can I interest you in a one of our kkwabaegi donuts? They're great for breakfast." The generic paper sack crinkled in between her fingers as she grabbed it from below the register. When had the lights in the shop gotten so bright? She squinted against them. "Or if you don't want something sweet, we have a cream cheese and garlic bread."

Gwydion blinked at her for a moment, then they raised one perfectly manicured hand and snapped their fingers. Everything stopped. The sounds of Heather in the back banging pans in the cramped kitchen, of Sarah's annoyingly impractical ankle boots on the gleaming black-and-white tile floor, of the buzzing ovens, of the city traffic outside—all of it stopped.

Gwydion looked around at everyone, frozen in place, and Darcie had just enough time to recognize that something truly weird and deeply unsettling was going on before Gwydion pinned her with an expression of dissatisfaction, one perfectly plucked brow lifted.

"You told me this would make you happy," they said, leaving no room for argument.

"I am happy." Darcie grit her teeth around the lie. She had never told Gwydion any such thing, she remembered that much. She'd simply said this was what she'd wanted. Her eyes flicked nervously to the people she could see over Gwydion's shoulder. Were they even breathing? She couldn't tell.

Gwydion's golden eyes narrowed, their too-red lips pressing into a line so thin that Darcie could only see the lip liner they'd used to keep their lipstick in place. "You. Are. Not. Happy."

"I am." Darcie lifted her chin, daring Gwydion to argue further. To tell her what it was she was feeling.

"I guess we'll just see about that, won't we?" Gwydion's eye twitched at one corner, their fingers already beginning to send sparks through the air.

"What're you doing?" Darcie jerked her hands away from where she'd been bracing herself on the counter. Her tennis shoes made a squeaking sound on the floor as she skidded back.

"Doing what I always do—Well. What I *should* always do. So sorry about steering you wrong the first time, child, I'll get it right this time." Gwydion nodded to themselves, a softness in their eyes that hadn't been there before. "Until you can learn to be honest with yourself and those around you about what you need and feel, anything you bake shall taste exactly as your mood was when you made it."

"What?" Darcie blinked, ignoring the tingling that spread from the tips of her fingers up her arms. Like when she'd rubbed her socks on the floor and touched the door-knob that one time.

"Hopefully, this will help you find real happiness," Gwydion said, looking sad. Then they were gone, leaving only a dusting of glitter in the air, and all the sound came rushing back at once. Darcie's ears popped.

"What does that even mean?!" Darcie shouted at the ceiling. All she earned for her trouble was several confused stares from her employees. She grunted, "Back to work. All of you!" and went to hide in the back office for the next hour, still not really sure what had happened.

TWO

Once the cat was out of the bag—*both literally and figuratively*, ze thought with no small amount of amusement—Hari Atsushi had found zirself dragged into a world of delightfully magical nonsense. Which spanned from a "third wheel" group chat with zir vet, Aura, and a literal fairy named Eero, to regular "family" dinners featuring a centuries old prince, a dragon, a mage, and zir bestie—and cousin—Yuuki.

"All I'm saying is if you're going to be late picking up ZhanZhan because you're going to a bakery for a 'work shoot,'" Aura said, and Hari could hear the air quotes through the phone. It wasn't that she didn't take zir work seriously, it was simply that Aura saw it for what it was: an excuse to eat yummy things, go fun places, and take pretty pictures. Really, Hari was living zir best life if ze did say so zirself. "You had better bring me back a pastry."

"Didn't Eero bring you lunch? He said in the chat he was going to—"

"That was hours ago, Hari! Do you know what time it is?" Aura huffed, and Hari could picture her puffing out her cheeks in irritation. It was positively adorable. Which ze wouldn't say on pain of the silent treatment from Eero.

"Two, I think." Hari shrugged, sidestepping a speed walking young businesswoman in heels. Zir camera bag thumped hard against zir thigh with the swift motion. "You know I don't really pay attention to the time."

Aura snorted on the other side of the line, and Hari could hear her tapping her pen impatiently against whatever file she'd been reading over when she called.

"Fine. I'll bring pastries for everyone. Happy?"

"Everyone?"

"Well, I can't play favorites." Hari pulled the phone away from zir face to double check the directions to Gyeong's. Another block. "Not if I don't want Eero to curse my coffee again," ze muttered.

"Oh my God, Hari. That was one time! We've talked about this!"

Hari winced. Ze'd hoped she wouldn't hear that. Ze put the phone back to zir ear, eyes narrowing to look for the shop's sign in the distance. There wasn't one, but there was a line winding its way down the block. *That* must be the place.

"Are you listening to me, Hari? I'm telling you, Eero and I aren't a thing. He's dating some pixie from the station now." Aura sounded almost put out about it, but Hari wasn't going to point that out to her. Her spiteful streak was worse than Eero's could ever be.

"I'm listening. I'm just not quite believing you, is all." Hari smiled to zirself, taking zir place at the back of the line.

"Not quite—" Aura hissed, smacking the file she'd been reading down on her desk loud enough that it slapped. "Not quite believing me. You sound just like Fable."

"I'll take that as—"

"That is *not* a compliment."

"Sounded like one to me." Hari grinned at the woman in front of zir, giving her a little wink. "Look, Aura, all I'm saying is you two have been dancing around each other for what . . . a year now? Maybe it's time you did something about it."

"He. Is. Dating. Someone. Else."

"Yeah, and if that isn't a cry for help, I've never seen one. Honestly? A pixie from the station? You believe that? Pixies are notoriously flammable." The woman in front of Hari had taken a step away from zir at the mention of pixies, and Hari rolled zir eyes, mouthing, 'Kids, right?'

"I've met her, she's very nice," Aura said primly.

"Right. What does Blaze say about all this?"

Aura mumbled something unintelligible into the phone that sounded like it had the word jellyfish in it. Maybe it was jealous and selfish? Hari couldn't be sure. Ze also decided ze didn't care. Whatever excuse Aura was making, it wasn't a valid one, and they both knew it.

"Well, if you don't make a move on him, I will. And we both know how that's going to end." Hari bit the inside of zir cheek to keep the smile from zir voice.

"You wouldn't!" Aura gasped.

"Wouldn't I?"

"I have a patient waiting for me. Bring pastries. We're not talking about this anymore." And then she hung up without so much as a goodbye.

"Brat." Hari huffed affectionately, zir pastel nails tapping against the glass as ze opened the camera app. Turning with zir back to the line, Hari pasted on a bright smile, pushed a lock of azure hair behind zir ear, and snapped a selfie. Zir nose wrinkled down at the picture; not zir best work, but it would do for a quick candid if ze slapped a filter on it.

The line moved up, and Hari moved with it, zir fingers typing out a caption.

> *Guess where I am and win a prize . . .*
>
> *My undying affection for being so awesome! And also maybe a coupon code for this rockin' eyeliner* 。 ●‿●。

"Have you been here before?" the woman in front of Hari asked when ze put zir phone away.

"Nope!" Hari popped the 'p', bouncing up onto zir toes to try to see over everyone's heads. "First time. Though I've heard a lot of great things about it."

She nodded, smiling a little. "Me either. It was in one of those articles online. Hidden Gems of New York or something like that."

"Really? Neat! I just heard about it from a couple of friends of mine." And by friends, ze meant people online who ze had never met but who always seemed to know the most exciting place to get sugary bliss at 2 p.m. on a Tuesday. "Did they have any pictures in the article? I tried to find it online, but their website is kind of outdated."

"Just one, I think. Hang on, I might still have it up." She pulled her phone from her purse and started flicking through what must have been dozens of articles about the city.

The line moved up again. Hari's hands raised, without thinking, for her shoulders. "Do you mind?" ze asked softly.

"Huh?" She looked at zir hands, and then up at the line, and laughed. "You're good. I can't do two things at once. Just give me a nudge when we move."

"Will do." Hari laughed, leading her forward by the shoulders and steering her around a dip in the sidewalk. "So, you aren't from around here?"

"Oh no. I'm visiting with my family. But they all wanted to go and see the Statue of Liberty." She wrinkled her nose, her eyes still focused on her screen. "It's too hot for all that today."

Hari nodded in understanding. "It is, but you probably should have gone. It's one of those things you've got to see at least once."

"Probably. We come every summer though, and I went last year. Ah! Here it is." She lifted her head, face lighting with victory, making her green eyes dance. *Cute.* She held out her phone to Hari, and ze frowned at the grainy stock photo they'd used for the article. The writer hadn't even bothered to take a shot with their phone for it.

"Well . . . that just won't do." Hari pulled out zir own phone and pulled up the article. Ze would have something to say to this blogger when ze got home about the proper etiquette for creating lists of tourist attractions.

"I'm kind of surprised the line is so long." She huffed, the air rustling the long bangs hanging in her eyes.

Hari nodded zir agreement, handing back her phone as ze did a quick search for Gyeong's on zir own phone. "It looks like it's been on a couple of lists, but they're all the same. No pictures. How weird. Maybe they've been in a magazine?"

"Maybe."

"Guess we're about to find out what's so special about it though, huh?" Hari grinned, nudging her forward again. "I'm Hari, by the way."

"Freya. Are you local?"

Hari nodded. "Born and raised! I actually grew up a few stations over."

"So you'd know all the best places to eat, wouldn't you?" Freya was practically giddy now, the emotion making her freckled cheeks dimple.

"Oh yeah, definitely. And shop. And party. If that's your thing." Hari winked, leaning back on zir heels and shoving zir hands into the oversized pockets of zir overalls.

Freya blushed, ducking her head. "So, ummm . . . could I get your number, and maybe you could show me some of those places?"

"What?!" Hari squeaked, overbalancing and knocking zir wide-brimmed felt hat askew. "Oh. No. I don't, umm . . . Oh look, the line's moving! It's time to go in!"

Freya blinked and turned to look at where the line had indeed headed inside. Her eyes caught on the array of pastries in the window, and that seemed to distract her enough that she forgot about Hari, to zir great relief. From there, Freya made a beeline for the front counter, and Hari turned to survey the shop.

It was . . . Well, Hari wasn't terribly impressed. Outdated would be putting it nicely. It was clean, yes, but not the cute, bright place that ze'd been expecting. Yellowed bulbs cast everything from the people to the pastries in a sickly yellow color. The laminate was peeling off the display cases, a dark finish making the whole place look that much darker. And the wrought iron tables were too small for more than one person, even if there were four dark wood chairs around each.

"Great. I knew I should have brought my lighting kit." Hari groaned, rocking back on zir heels again. Closing zir eyes and taking a deep breath, Hari looked around for the best workaround. "Let's see . . . "

If ze moved a table toward the front window, it would get plenty of natural light. And then there would be the backdrop of the well-lit pastries in the window display, and the city street beyond. It wasn't ideal, but it was certainly better than . . . the rest of the place.

"Right." Hari nodded. "This is going to take a little longer than I'd like."

Hari pulled out zir phone to fire off another text to Aura, letting her know that she could send ZhanZhan home with Fable. Ze'd have to owe her a pastry. Probably more than one. Maybe ze could con Eero into picking up some cronuts from that bakery near the station for the whole office. That would keep Aura off Hari's case for at least a day or so.

Scrubbing at the fuzzy edge of zir undercut, Hari made zir way to the register. The menu above the counter was . . . It was a lot. There had to be at least fifty different varieties of pastry, each with a description beneath it in text too tiny for Hari to read, even with zir glasses.

The girl behind the counter yawned into the back of her wrist before pulling a generic brown paper sack from beneath the counter. "What can I get you?"

"Ummm . . . " Hari huffed, rolling zir eyes. "How about you get me whatever your favorite is. What's that?"

The girl blinked at zir, a bored expression making her lids heavy.

"All right then. How about just get me your five best-selling items."

Another slow blink. Like a bunny who was quickly losing interest in the person in front of them and about to bound off to do something more exciting. Likely knock over the trash, in Hari's experience.

Hari let out a breath, rubbing the bridge of zir nose, and

although it physically pained Hari to do so, ze pulled out zir phone and listed the things in the article the blogger had recommended. They would no doubt be awful, as the things recommended in such articles were usually chosen based on some arbitrary popularity scale, not on actual taste, but there wasn't much else Hari could do.

THREE

Darcie was pulling a pan of red bean buns from the oven when there was a loud scraping sound from the front. She just managed to set the tray down without dropping a single bun before hastily wiping her hands on a towel and heading out the swinging doors of the kitchen.

"What are you all doing up here?! We're in the middle of a—" Darcie stopped mid snap when she saw where the girls were looking. Someone in a pair of sloppily fashionable overalls and a floppy hat, with long cobalt blue hair tied back into a loose braid, had dragged one of their tables over to the window. Darcie blinked, watching as the person shifted things around on the table, then stood on one of the chairs.

With a huff, Darcie dropped the towel onto the counter and marched across the shop to where the person had bent over with a large camera clasped carefully between their long fingers. The person must have seen her out of the corner of their eye, because they didn't turn to look at her as they asked, "Do you guys happen to have any branded napkins or something?"

"Branded napkins?" Darcie frowned, arms crossed over her chest, as she glared up at the person on the chair. The other patrons were doing their best not to stare as the line moved sluggishly toward the counter.

"Yeah. Like with the logo and the bakery name on it. You know, like they do at Siren Coffee?" the person asked absently, shifting on the chair to rearrange their bun on the plain paper sack it had come in again. "No, it's still not quite right," they muttered to themselves. More fiddling, the sack crinkling loudly in the pointed silence of the bakery. "Honestly, this would be so much better if they weren't brown. Have you ever thought about white pastry bags? Everything stands out so much better against white."

"This is not *Siren Coffee*," Darcie snapped.

The person's head jerked to look at Darcie, darkly lined brown eyes widening a fraction at the curt tone as they lowered their camera. "Excuse me?"

"I said, this isn't Siren Coffee." Darcie felt oddly pinned down by the intensity in that light brown stare. She'd been expecting frivolity and carelessness, from the way they were dressed. Just another hipster trying to make a name for themselves. But this person . . . They looked serious. Maybe they weren't in a suit and heels, but there was something polished and professional about them. Not their clothes, surely, or the artistic cat eye penciled about their eyes but in their gaze itself. As if they were constantly assessing the world around them and looking for ways to make it brighter, prettier, more social media friendly. Playing a game of chicken with the algorithm and winning.

"I am aware this isn't Siren Coffee," they said plainly, still not bothering to get down from the chair where they towered over Darcie.

"Get off the chair."

"What? Why?" They blinked, looking down at where their grubby black Converse were still perched neatly atop the chair that Appa had so carefully selected two decades ago.

"Because it's a safety hazard! You could fall and hurt yourself and then sue us for your own idiocy!" Darcie wished suddenly she hadn't tied her short hair back in a ponytail to work; she could feel the pointed stares of the other customers.

More blinking, and then they laughed, a bright burbling sound that filled the quiet space with the warmth of freshly baked muffins. They bent over further, clutching their camera to their stomach as they continued to laugh, eyes squeezed shut. Darcie's face felt unbearably hot.

The soft chortles faded eventually, and they straightened before jumping down from the chair to stand right in front of Darcie—too close, even closer than arm's length—with their hand outstretched. "I'm Hari."

Darcie's hands clenched into fists where they were tucked behind her elbows. "What are you doing here?"

Hari laughed nervously as they tucked their hands back into their pockets, their camera dangling from their neck. "I run Hari's Hair-Raising Finds."

"What?"

"It's a blog. Well . . . blog, Viewtube channel, social media accounts, oh, and I'm getting into that new one . . . What was it called?" Hari hummed, fingers drumming on their chin. "Ah well, point being, I'm an influencer, after a fashion."

"And it's called—"

"Hari's Hair-Raising Finds. Yup" Hari popped the 'p', their face brightening into a blinding smile. Darcie squinted to keep her retinas from burning.

"That's a stupid name," Darcie said, without really thinking before the words left her lips. It was rude. She'd never been rude to a customer before. Short, maybe. But never rude. She wasn't sure why she was being rude now. There was just something about Hari that set her teeth on edge. It was the outfit, she decided, it was just so . . . *cute*. Or maybe it was the encounter with Gwydion that morning. Either way, Darcie had had enough of people in general.

Hari laughed, their hand scrubbing at the soft looking black stubble of their undercut. "Yeah, it's kinda silly. But to be fair, I was twenty-one, and my little sister picked it out."

"You couldn't change it?"

"You haven't met my little sister." Hari snickered, stuffing their hands back into their pockets. Darcie stared. Because what else was she going to do? Not stare? Go back to the kitchen and slam the ovens shut so hard that the one with the rusted hinge finally gave up and the door fell off? No. She was going to stare. Like a creeper. "So . . . about the napkins. Or even if you had a business card maybe?"

"What do you need it for?"

"For pictures." Hari pulled out their phone, quick fingers flying across the screen until they'd opened a social media account. They held it up for Darcie to see. The profile picture was a tiny round image of Hari with bright green hair drinking an even brighter green cocktail. Darcie wondered if they'd dyed their hair to match for that specific shoot. Probably.

"This is what you do for a living?" Darcie asked, unable to keep the incredulity from her voice. She wasn't sure why she sounded that way. It wasn't like this was the first time she was hearing about influencers. She knew what they were. It's just . . . well . . . she'd never really taken them seriously was all. It had always sounded like an easy way to get free stuff. But Hari hadn't asked for anything free. In fact, they'd bought the pastries themselves. A welcome consideration for a small business.

"It keeps ZhanZhan and YingYing in bok choy." Hari shrugged. "And I'm good at it."

"ZhanZhan and YingYing?"

"My rabbits! They have their own accounts too. Hang on." Hari pulled the phone back into themselves and tapped a couple more times on the screen. "We partnered with this lady who makes pet sweaters a couple months ago. They were the cutest thing *ever*. Even my sister said so, and she hates rabbits. Well. 'Hate' is a strong word. She calls them rodents. She'd rather have a dog, she says. But we can't have dogs because I—"

"Out." Darcie felt everyone in the shop stop again, their heads whipping around to look at her.

"What?" Hari looked up from their phone, lips pressed into a confused frown. "What do you mean 'out'?"

"I mean get out. Take your pastries and go."

"Now look. I'm doing you a favor here. There's no need to be rude about it." Hari straightened up, their phone tucked back into their pocket as they lifted their chin. "All I asked for was a little something to make it more obvious where I was. You don't even have a sign out front. Just the name decal on the window. How are people supposed to know you're here if you don't do any work to get yourself out there? This is New York for Pete's sake. If you don't put forth a little effort, you're going to go under in a . . . well, in a New York minute."

"We are doing just fine." Darcie bit the words out, her short nails digging into her palms where her fists clenched even tighter. She resisted the urge to point to the line that was still out the door. It would be rude.

"Well yeah, now you are. But what about—"

"You're wasting my time," Darcie hissed. "I have a business to run. I can't be wasting time playing on my phone."

Hari's expression twisted, their brown eyes hardened. "Fine," they said, stuffing their camera into their bag.

"Fine."

"Fine!" Hari grabbed their pastry bags and spun on their heel for the door.

"Fine!" Darcie stomped after them, her chest heaving with irritation. The crowed parted to let them through to the door.

"Fine!" The chime above the door jingled merrily, and then Hari yanked it shut behind them.

"Fine!"

"Uh . . . boss?" Sarah asked.

"What?"

"I think they're gone."

"Well good! Get back to work! All of you!" Darcie turned to drag the table back to where it'd been, wiping away the crumbs left behind by Hari's pastries, and then headed back into the back, still pointedly ignoring the sting of judgmental gazes on the back of her neck, where she promptly flopped into her chair and covered her face with her hands to smother a scream.

WITH THE ENCOUNTERS with Gwydion and Hari in the rearview, everything went back to normal. Or it seemed to, anyway. Darcie lost herself again to the push and pull of

dough, the buzz of the oven timers, and the constant mutter-
ings of customers. The low hum of drudgery that she had
gotten so used to, she hardly felt it anymore.

It wasn't until a week later, as she was loading a fresh
tray of sweet rice cakes onto the cooling rack, that she finally
understood the damage she'd done.

"Boss," the girl working the counter said.

"What is it?" Darcie slid the tray into its spot and made
her way over.

"We had a return."

"A what? You can't return a pastry. It's not a sweater."
Darcie frowned at the woman on the other side of the
counter. She was shorter, her hair long over her shoulders
and a pair of dark-rimmed glasses perched on her nose.
"What's wrong with it?"

"It's got too much salt in it." The woman nudged the
paper sack across the counter toward Darcie. "Try it yourself. It's like you used salt instead of sugar."

"That's impossible. I made those myself. And we have
all the recipes up on the walls in the back. No one could
have made that mistake." Still, she tore off a piece of the
bun, popping it into her mouth to give it an experimental
chew. It was fine at first, exactly how it should be, then she
bit into it, teeth tearing at the delicate skin and . . . She
coughed, choking as the salt threatened to burn away all the
moisture in her throat.

"See?"

"I'm so sorry about that. Give her a full refund. I'll grab
the tray and toss them. We'll have to make another batch."

The woman nodded, pleased. "You know, when Hari
put up that review, I was skeptical. I'm glad ze seemed to
just be having a bad day."

"Review?" Darcie coughed into her fist as she scooped what was left of the bun into the bin behind the counter.

"Yeah. Hari posted last week, I think, that ze had the worst customer service here. Something about a run-in with the owner. It was so unlike zir, I just couldn't understand it. Everyone loves Hari."

"Right. Everyone," Darcie mumbled. "Can you show me the review?"

"Sure!" The woman smiled, tapping away at her phone with the faint clickety-clack of fake nails. "Here."

She slid the phone across the counter, and Darcie leaned over to get a better look. It was a blog, Hari's blog, Darcie supposed, considering the header read 'Hari's Hair-Raising Finds'.

With a line out the door, and a steady stream of customers, it would seem as if Gyeong's bakery in K-town has something special, and that assumption would be correct.

The red bean buns were absolutely magical. I haven't had any that good since my trip to Seoul last year. My only regret is that the atmosphere of Gyeong's is both outdated and hostile. After a small run-in with one of Gyeong's owners, who was perhaps just having a bad day, I myself will not be returning. However, I encourage you to go and try your luck. If nothing else, the pastries were definitely worth it!

Until next time, happy hunting.

Hari ●⌣⌐

Darcie blinked down at the review for a moment longer and let out a breath. The picture Hari had used was on a white marble counter and made the bun in question look mouth-wateringly good. It would seem ze really had a knack for it after all.

"Thank you."

"Yup!" The woman grinned. "I'll stop back by next week to try again, all right?"

"Sure." Darcie nodded. She felt strangely hollowed out, her shoulders slumping forward. That review had been . . . well it wasn't exactly complimentary. But she supposed it wasn't horrible either. With the audience Hari had, things could have been worse.

FOUR

"You were too nice," Alrik said, frowning down at his phone. He still struggled with the lack of buttons, even a year later, but Hari was surprised how quickly he'd adapted to the new technology. It would seem that although one couldn't teach an old dog new tricks, one could in fact teach an old cat new tricks. Well, prince turned cat turned man . . . as it were. Hari bit down on a snicker. "That girl practically threw you out of her shop, and you praised her food."

"It was really good." Hari shrugged, clicking zir chopsticks softly around a bit of still crunchy bok choy stem. "Seriously, if her personality weren't so . . ."

"Abhorrent?"

"I didn't say that."

"You didn't have to."

Hari frowned, zir eyes flicked to Yuuki for backup. Ze knew that Alrik was just trying to be supportive and protective of someone he saw as family, but that didn't make it any easier to explain to him why Hari couldn't be so uncharitable with zir review of Gyeong's.

"Alrik, be nice." Yuuki chided softly, picking a piece of chicken out of his ramen to set on top of Alrik's noodles while Alrik grabbed a collection of chives to add to Yuuki's bowl. "Let Hari finish."

"Fine. Finish." Alrik rolled his bright green eyes up into the unkempt black hair hanging over his forehead.

"Well for one," Hari said around a mouth full of noodles that earned zir a disgusted scoff from Alrik and a soft chuckle from Yuuki. Ze swallowed them down with a gulp. "My blog isn't like that. The whole vibe is very upbeat."

"Then why not just skip reviewing it?" Yuuki asked, although Hari was sure he already knew the answer. He was just trying to get this conversation over as quickly as possible. Hari was grateful. They had other things to talk about. Happier things. Things that didn't involve a stuck-up, pretentious, arrogant baker.

"Because I'd already posted about it on my accounts. People were expecting a review, so they got one. Now, if we're all done interrogating Hari, can we get down to the important discussion? The reason why we are all gathered here today is to welcome Alrik to the family and to make him an offer he can't—"

"This isn't the mob, Hari. Stop it." Katsuko rolled her eyes, because that's what little sisters did when their older sibling was being ridiculous. Hari didn't hold it against her. Thus was the nature of having siblings.

"Isn't it?"

"You are the absolute worst. Tell me why I had to be here for this."

"Because you love us, KitKat. That's why." Yuuki leaned across the table to take Katsuko's cheeks in his hands and give them an affectionate smoosh.

"So I didn't have to be here by myself with these two,"

Alrik deadpanned, reaching over to swat Yuuki's hands away from Katsuko's face. "Stop that. Last time you did that, she bit you."

"You make my baby sister sound like some kind of rabid porcupine." Hari snickered into zir hand, not making any move to stop Yuuki as he tugged at Katsuko's full cheeks.

"Isn't she?" Alrik gave Yuuki's wrists another tug and managed to get him to let go of Katsuko.

"Hey!" Katsuko huffed, rubbing at her reddened cheeks. "I'm not rabid."

"Of course you aren't. My cute little porcupine." Hari pinched Katsuko's cheek closest to zir, laughing when she yelped and swatted zir away. "Plus, I needed video evidence of this to send back to mama, since she couldn't make it."

"Yuuki, can you just ask zir? Please? So we can get these two out of our apartment?" Alrik glared at Hari, who just grinned back cheekily. Honestly, it was so easy to get him riled.

"Ooooh, get out the camera. Get out the camera." Hari swatted Katsuko's arm with the back of zir hand in several quick thumps. Katsuko grumbled but pulled up the video feature on her phone and started recording.

"You ready?" Yuuki asked. His voice had gone wobbly suddenly, a soft flush painting his cheeks. And it was so unbelievably cute, Hari wanted to scream, but didn't because that would have ruined the moment.

Katsuko nodded.

"Right then." Yuuki took a deep breath, as if he didn't already know the answer, as if he were nervous. Hari wondered how he'd ever managed to propose to Alrik and wished, not for the first time, that they'd gotten a video of *that*. But it had been a small, private thing. A dinner with just the two of them, much like this one. And Yuuki, unlike

Hari, didn't feel the need to keep a running record of his entire life. They'd done one very cute selfie after the fact, but that had been it.

"You got this, Yuuki." Katsuko whispered, giving him a thumbs up over the top of her phone.

Yuuki laughed and let it out in a rush. "Will you be my best person, Hari?"

"Yes!" Hari leaped across the low table, flinging zir arms around Yuuki in a tight hug. "Oh, you two are going to have such a wonderful wedding. It's going to be so cute. And KitKat and I are going to get so many beautiful photos. And there are going to be so many happy memories. And . . . Wait . . . Who's Alrik's best person?"

"Gwydion." Alrik worked his chopsticks into his bowl to pick up a mouthful of noodles. "Seemed appropriate."

Hari saw Katsuko shift out of the corner of zir eye, lowering her phone and going back to her food.

"Hmm, then I'm going to need something truly fabulous to wear." Hari kissed Yuuki's cheek and slid back down to the floor on the other side of the table, ignoring the bit of broth ze'd spilled onto the wood and zir sweater. "Katsuko, make a list."

"I'm not your secretary." Katsuko rolled her eyes, but her fingers were already typing. "A suit, I think"

"Yes. A suit. A tux, rather. Maybe in velvet. I can't have Gwydion outshining me." Hari tapped zir fingers on zir jaw thoughtfully. "Maybe a green. Or a deep red. Or . . . What's your color scheme?"

"Oh . . . uh . . . " Yuuki shifted, his face flushed again. "That's the other thing."

Hari's head tilted, hair falling into zir eyes. "What?"

"We need help planning it. Gwydion offered, but they're so busy with the book tour that it just didn't feel right. And Yuuki and I have the food truck." Alrik had set his chopsticks down against the ceramic purple rest beside his matching bowl and took a breath. "So we need a hand with finding vendors and keeping everything in order. We can't afford a planner."

"Say no more." Hari held up zir hand to stop him. "I've got this covered. KitKat, they'll need flowers, a caterer, a cake, suits, an officiate, a venue . . . Do you have a venue?"

"We're doing it at Crystal Tokyo." Yuuki's shoulders relaxed, slouching back a little where he was seated on a pillow. "We're thinking soft colors."

"Hmm. I can work with that. Katsuko, make a note."

"I'm not your secretary," Katsuko huffed again, but Hari could hear her fingers tapping against her screen. "Email or text?"

"Email. Mark it as urgent. I need to get started right away. With a venue out of the way, we should start looking at caterers and cakes as soon as possible. Those will likely be the hardest things to choose."

"Sage said she'd handle the catering as her gift. That's taken care of." Yuuki slurped from his bowl and then moved to gather up his and Alrik's.

"I've got that. You stay and plot with your cousins," Alrik said swatting Yuuki's hands away and gathering up their dishes to head for the kitchen.

"It's not plotting!" Hari called after him, a smirk tugging at zir lips.

"Whatever you say."

"I have a list of bakeries I'd like to try for cakes already." Yuuki pulled out his phone and slid it across to Hari. "The bakers are all very reputable, well known in the food scene. I figured . . . if there's one thing we don't want to skimp on, it's that."

Zir eyes flicked down, and then ze stopped, frowning. "Gyeong's?"

Yuuki shrugged sheepishly. "The matcha roll cake was really good. I think that flavor as a wedding cake would be perfect."

Hari snorted. "Yeah. Sure." But ze had a feeling that this wasn't just about a cake. It was about something else. "Let's try the other places first, all right?"

"Of course!" Yuuki beamed.

FAMILY DINNER WAS a couple of days later, and that's when Hari's suspicions were confirmed.

"I really don't think this is wise," Alrik's voice carried down the hall of Hari's miraculously spacious two-bedroom. Eero had said ze must have had the luck of a leprechaun finding it, but Hari wasn't sure whether it was that or zir unique ability to smile zir way into people's good graces. Maybe a combination of both.

"I'm with Alrik. This is a bad idea. It was bad enough that Gwydion butted in with us. We shouldn't be encouraging them to do it with someone else. Especially someone who they haven't cursed." Another voice grumbled—Blaze, Hari's mind supplied for zir, conjuring up the scarred, snarling face of the firefighting dragon. An oxymoron, Hari had thought when ze'd first met Blaze, but then ze had gotten to know him and realized it made sense.

"I don't see the harm," Fable said, tone soft but firm as it often was when dealing with an unruly pet owner, a scared dog, or Blaze. Funny how those things were so similar.

"Fable's right, it can't hurt. The worst that could happen is they—" Yuuki spun, pressing his face into ZhanZhan's white fur to smother the rest of his words. ZhanZhan's ear twitched, his beady rabbit eyes looking up at Hari in a bored, unimpressed expression.

"Is what? The worst that could happen is what?" Hari asked, bending to scoop up YingYing when the black rabbit came barreling toward zir. "What's Gwydion plotting?"

"A meet cute." Fable shifted beside Blaze. Yuuki turned to glare at him but didn't say anything.

"With the baker," Blaze added, not even looking a little bit uncomfortable with throwing Gwydion under the bus. Which was completely fair, considering what Gwydion had done to him in particular, in Hari's mind. "Gwydion cursed the baker. Dorothy, or Dorcas, or whatever."

"Darcie," Fable corrected softly.

"What?" Hari jerked as YingYing wriggled to be let down again. Ze crouched, putting the rabbit gently back on the ground where it promptly took off like a bat out of hell, followed closely by ZhanZhan.

No one said anything for a second that seemed to stretch on into forever. And then the timer on the oven dinged, and Yuuki leaped to his feet. "Dinner's ready!"

Hari's eyes narrowed on zir cousin, lips pressed into a hard line. Yuuki was hiding something. More than just Gwydion plotting a meet cute. Yuuki knew something that was going to make Hari angry, and Hari didn't think ze liked the correlation between Gwydion's decision and Yuuki's sudden avoidance. That could only mean one thing: Gwydion was planning to set *Hari* up with the snotty baker.

"So, what's the baker's curse?" Hari asked, pulling out zir chair to settle at the table.

"What?" Yuuki stopped where he was spooning rice onto Alrik's plate.

"Blaze said Gwydion cursed the baker. What's their curse? And why?"

"We didn't ask." Fable's voice was even, but he suddenly became very interested in his glass of water.

"We did ask," Blaze scoffed, rolling his eyes. "But Gwydion wouldn't tell us. They do that sometimes, get all shifty."

"They weren't being shifty." Yuuki huffed, flopping a healthy spoonful of the fragrant yellow rice onto his own plate. "They just don't think it's anyone's business but the one who was cursed. It's up to that person to share it."

"*Why* were they cursed?" Hari hated repeating zirself, but this seemed as important, if not more, than the curse itself.

"Oh, something about not knowing true happiness if it bit her." Alrik waved his hand with a flourish, a gesture Hari had seen Gwydion do one too many times. "If you're so interested, why don't you ask Gwydion?"

"I'm not—" Hari squeaked and then cleared zir throat to push the sound away. "I'm not interested."

"Sure, you aren't." Blaze smirked over the rim of his glass.

"Either way, if you were, Gwydion is just a phone call away." Fable was smiling the smile of someone who thought they knew something no one else did. Hari didn't like it. Nor did ze like the subtle heat that had crawled up the back of zir neck. Thank goodness for long hair.

"Or a shout." Blaze shrugged. "Provided they aren't busy."

"They're always busy when you call." Alrik bit back a chuckle.

"They are not! I could call right now, and they'd show up. Bet."

Fable and Yuuki snickered and didn't say a word as Alrik and Blaze descended into a bickering match that had both ZhanZhan and YingYing avoiding the dining room on pain of death.

ZE HAD DEBATED it back and forth for hours after the others had left. Hari knew it wasn't a good idea. Ze knew ze should just stay out of it. If the owner of Gyeong's was cursed, that was her problem, not Hari's. Yet, as ze lay in bed, staring up at the ceiling, the sound of YingYing munching on a piece of crunchy lettuce in zir ear, Hari couldn't get the baker's face out of zir mind. Ze needed to know.

"Gwydion," Hari called to the streetlight-striped ceiling. Ze only half expected an answer. After all, Gwydion was likely too busy.

There was no sound, just a shimmering curtain of glitter and starlight as Gwydion materialized on the foot of Hari's bed. They were dressed in a neon blue pantsuit, one leg crossed over the other, foot tapping through the air in a matching patent leather shoe.

Hari blinked, wide-eyed, then slowly pushed zirself up to lean against the headboard. "You came."

"I always do, sweetheart." They winked and let out a soft chuckle. "Now, what is it you need?"

"I just . . . " Hari took a breath. Was ze losing zir nerve? That was ridiculous. Hari never lost zir nerve. "I just wanted to know about the curse."

"Which one, sugar? You'll have to be more specific. There are a lot of them floating around out there." Gwydion wriggled their fingers through the air, the light from outside bouncing off the sparkles on their nail polish. "You mean the baker, don't you?"

"Yeah, the baker."

"Do you like her?"

"No!" Hari choked on the word. "She's . . . she's . . . "

"She's very unhappy," Gwydion said, their voice strangely softened by some emotion that Hari couldn't exactly identify. "I just don't think she realizes it yet."

"How can someone not realize they're unhappy?"

Gwydion sighed, leaning back on their hands. "It's like boiling a frog."

"Why would you boil a frog?"

"Not the point, child. Now listen." Gwydion rolled their eyes. "The point is, if you crank the heat right away, the frog will leap out of the pot. But if you turn the heat up little by little, before the frog even realizes what's going on, they're boiled alive."

"So she's just . . . slowly gotten more and more unhappy over time?"

"No. More like it happened all at once, but she was so distracted by something else that she didn't see it. And now she's just there. This is just how she feels, all the time. She's just a boiled frog."

"That doesn't make any sense." Hari frowned.

"It's been my experience that most human beings don't, kiddo." Gwydion shook their head. "All I'm saying is give her a chance, yeah? You might be surprised."

"So I *am* the meet cute."

"Well, of course you are!" Gwydion laughed. "I mean, you've already stuck yourself into her story. I'd be fool to not use what's in front of me."

"I'm not dating her." Hari knew exactly how petulant that sounded and ze didn't care.

Gwydion shrugged. "I'm not a matchmaker, sugar. I just put people together who can help one another." Hari wasn't sure what zir face was doing, but whatever it was, it must have been skeptical, because Gwydion said, "I think you and Darcie Alston can learn something from each other. That's all."

Then without another word, the witch disappeared, leaving behind a patch of glitter on Hari's bedding. "Great, now I'm going to have to wash that."

FIVE

It didn't make sense. None of it made sense. Darcie had been making every recipe on Gyeong's menu since she was old enough to stand on a step stool in the kitchen and help eomma. She had them memorized forward, backward, and in between. She knew which ones could be modified if they were out of an ingredient and which ones couldn't. She'd even helped eomma create some of them. She had never in her life—

"It doesn't taste like anything," the man said, his nose twisting up in disgust. "Literally nothing. I don't even know how that's possible. Everything has to taste like something!"

"I'm so sorry about that. Would you like to try something else?" the other Sarah asked.

"No. I want my money back."

The other Sarah glanced to Darcie. Darcie nodded. Then she grabbed the tray of roll cakes from the display case and disappeared into the back. Let the girls deal with customers for a while; she needed to know what the hell was going on.

Her hands shook. Her hands hadn't shaken since

eomma had passed. Darcie growled, tightening them into fists. She would figure this out. She had to. Eomma had always said that the best way to understand what had gone wrong with a recipe was to try it.

She grabbed a tray from the cooling rack and made her way back out front to collect one of every pastry from the display case. The other Sarah cut her a look but didn't say anything, for which Darcie was grateful. She didn't want to explain that she had either forgotten how to make all of the recipes eomma had taught her or was clearly having some kind of nervous breakdown. The breakdown was more likely; she'd never forget the recipes. They were burned into her, with every scorched fingertip and scar lingering from a too-hot oven door, a part of her as nothing else had ever been.

The metal stool scraped against the tile loudly as she dragged it to the big worktable in the center. Sucking in another breath, she grabbed a slice of roll cake and started to eat.

Nothing. Just as the man had said. There was nothing. No flavor at all. Which was arguably impossible. Everything had to taste like something.

She grabbed a mochi bun and bit into it. The texture was perfect, chewy, just how it should have been. But again, nothing.

Next, a crispy fried kkwabaegi donut, soft and doughy on the inside. Nothing.

Fluffy and moist milk bread. Nothing.

Doughy dasik cookies. Nothing.

Nothing. Nothing. And more nothing. No sweetness of sugar. No tang of filling. No hint of any of the flavor and life that always went into eomma's recipes. Even the newer ones, the ones Darcie had helped to create when she'd been old enough to understand how flavor worked.

Darcie sniffed, scrubbing at her eyes. When had she started crying? She wasn't sure. But the tears dripped down in a soft patter onto the cold steel of the worktable. They slid salty against the absence of flavor on her lips.

It didn't make sense. None of it made sense. How was that even possible. She'd . . . she'd just have to make them again. Yes, that's what she'd have to do. Scrubbing away the tears on the sleeve of her shirt, she stood.

"Sarah!" she called to the girl at the register, who blinked at her, confused. Maybe Sarah wasn't her name after all? Darcie shook her head. It didn't matter. "We're closing up early."

Probably-not-Sarah's mouth fell open, then she scuttled after Darcie into the kitchen. "Closing up early, why?"

"I'm making everything from scratch. We can't sell any of these. Clear out the cases, we'll start fresh in the morning." Determination and anger had lit itself like a fire in Darcie's belly. She tightened her apron around her waist and moved to slide everything off the worktable into the bin.

"What?"

"You and the other girls can take the rest of the day off. I'll do this on my own." Darcie nodded to herself, satisfied at the freshly cleaned worktable, and went to gather ingredients.

"Don't you want . . . help?"

"No. No. I've got it. You all go on home. I can do this." A mixing bowl clattered against steel. Darcie tugged the recipe for roll cake off the wall and slapped it down beside her bowl. She'd follow it exactly. No chance of mis-remembering that way.

Probably-not-Sarah looked at the table full of ingredients, then the likely slightly crazed look on Darcie's face, and just said, "Umm . . . Okay."

Then she and the others made themselves scarce, and all that was left was the sound of mixing ingredients. Darcie lost herself to it. Lost herself to the sour, determined, angry feeling in her gut that said she'd prove them wrong. That she'd figure out what was happening and she'd fix it.

The first thing to come out of the oven was the roll cake. Darcie rolled it into a neat swirl while it was still hot, setting it aside while she prepared the filling and a dough for buns that would need to rise. Once those were done, she moved to slather cream on the rolled cake and cut it into even slices.

"All right, Darcie, you've got this. You followed the recipe exactly. This should be perfect. Just like eomma's." She didn't even bother with a fork, just picked up the slice and took a big bite . . . Which she immediately regretted when something bitter hit her palette. Her jaw clenched, eyes watering, as she fought to choke it down. The sugar sat like lead in her stomach.

Again.

She scrubbed at her eyes and started from scratch.

Hours later, it was the same roll cake. The same cream. The same ingredients. This time, the clinging taste of desperation stuck to her tongue. It was bitter, though not as bitter as before, with a sour note of curdled milk.

Maybe the milk had gone bad. She went to the fridge, took out the jug, and gave it a careful sniff. It didn't smell sour. She went to the cabinet and pulled down a measuring cup, pouring a little of the milk into it then sipping from it. It was fine.

"I don't . . . I don't understand." Darcie dropped onto the stool hard enough to jolt her tail bone, but she hardly noticed. "I followed the recipe exactly. The ingredients are fine. What . . . what is it?!"

"It's you," a voice said from across the worktable. Darcie's head jerked up to meet Gwydion's golden eyes. They were dressed in a silk pajama set, deep green with polka dots. Their long red hair was woven in a neat braid, which was carelessly slung over their shoulder.

"What?"

"It's you. You're the reason everything is coming out wrong. I told you, your baking reflects your emotions. That one," Gwydion pointed to the cake that had tasted like nothing, "you baked while you were just going through the motions. You didn't feel anything at all when you made it, did you?"

"What?"

"This one." A perfectly manicured nail tapped against the metal. "You were angry, weren't you? Furious that you'd been getting so many complaints. That's why it's bitter."

"I don't understand." That was a lie; she did understand. It just didn't make sense. Nothing about this made sense.

"And that last? That's what desperation tastes like."

"What are you saying?!"

"Tell me, Darcie . . . " Gwydion leaned on the table, flour gathering at the elbows of their pajamas. "When was the last time you baked something because you were excited to make it? When was the last time you baked something for the sheer joy of creation?"

"I have a business to run!" It was a weak excuse; Darcie knew it as soon as the words left her lips. Eomma had loved baking every day. She had spent her life perfecting old recipes and making new ones. She had found the joy in every single bun or cake. Darcie . . . Darcie didn't have that luxury. "This isn't . . . It's not for fun."

Gwydion stared at her, expression blank. Then they shrugged. "Suit yourself. But I told you what was going to happen. Either you figure out how to be happy again or everything you make is going to taste . . . like this."

"I am happy." The lie sat heavy on her tongue.

Gwydion didn't say anything, they just continued to watch Darcie, judgement sitting in their eyes. And honestly, that was worse. So much worse than if they'd just said what they were thinking. Gwydion sighed, and Darcie saw it more than she heard it, their shoulders slumping and their face turning sad. Then they disappeared, leaving behind a cloud of glitter that would no doubt ruin everything it touched.

"I am happy." The protest was too weak and too late for Gwydion to have believed it. Darcie huffed. "And now I have to vacuum!"

She should have gone home. She should have called it a night. She should have packed it up. But there were still all the pastries for the next day to make and the kitchen to clean up. And she knew she wouldn't be able to sleep. Not after everything that had happened. So she set to work.

Hours and hours later, there were three more roll cakes, four batches of mochi buns, and two loaves of milk bread.

"Empty," she whispered poking at the latest loaf of milk bread. It jiggled a little, exactly the right texture. But she knew what she'd taste if she cut off a slice to try it. Nothing. It would be *empty*. It would be devoid of flavor, of meaning, of life. Just like her. Just like her life. Because she'd somehow managed to take the thing her eomma had loved the most and suck the soul right out of it.

"Because that's what you do Darcie. You suck the soul out of things. You're like some real-life version of a dement—"

"Boss?" Heather poked her head into the kitchen. There was a pair of sunglasses in her long dark hair, holding it back from her face, and a pastry bag in her hand with logo on it Darcie didn't recognize. "Are you all right back here? The girls said they heard groaning."

"Fine." Darcie pressed the lie past her teeth with her tongue when it tried to stick at the back of her throat like bubble gum. She wasn't fine. She'd likely never be fine again. Because the truth was, she'd made a choice. And it was that she wasn't going to bake anymore. For the sake of the business, she was going to let the girls handle it. "Can you and the girls get everything baked for the day?"

Heather blinked perfectly lined eyes at Darcie. "But . . . boss. We open in a couple hours."

"I know, just do what you can. I'll work on getting every-thing else set up for open." Darcie stood, stretched, and headed to the office to get the cash drawer. When she made her way out front to take down the chairs and set up the register, there was a little white paper sack with a delicate rose-shaped pastry sitting on the counter. "Heather, what's this?"

Heather poked her head out to grin at Darcie. "It's from the new bakery a few blocks over. They just opened last month, but they're doing pretty well. They make the cutest buns I've ever seen!"

Darcie turned the bag over to get a better look at the bakery's logo. It was a lily, pressed onto the paper with a stamp that had smudged just enough to let people know that that too had been done by hand. Personalized, in a small, impersonal way. But that wasn't what bothered Darcie about it. What bothered her was that she recognized that lily. She'd seen it over and over again. Sketched onto thick paper, doodled on the sides of class notes, even tattooed onto the paper-thin skin of a delicate wrist.

"What's it called?" She thought she knew already, but she had to make sure. She had to hear it.

"Huh?"

"The bakery, what's it called?"

"Oh. Stargazer's."

Ssregi.

SIX

There was one bakery left on the list. Just one. Hari and Yuuki had spent a month going down the list whenever Yuuki had an afternoon that he could spare, and Hari had pushed Gyeong's to the very end in the hopes that they could avoid it altogether. There couldn't be a meet cute if ze didn't show up, right?

Yuuki had marked several off, and the list of potentials was down to not more than a handful. Hari didn't see why they couldn't pick from one of them, but Yuuki was being . . . stubborn. Which wasn't terribly unusual for him but was still annoying.

"I don't really have time this afternoon . . . " Yuuki shifted on the other side of the phone, and Hari could hear Alrik in the background taking someone's order from the window of their food truck. "You could go without me, I trust you."

"Yeah, that's not happening." Hari rearranged the stack of books ze was working with on zir workstation. Ze wondered if Yuuki's reluctance to participate was Gwydion-sanctioned or something else, then quickly shrugged it off. "The appointment is at four. The lunch rush should definitely be over by then."

"Yeah, but then there's the prep work for tomorrow. It's a Saturday, you know how Saturdays are."

Hari sighed, adjusting the light above the table and stepping back to get a better look at the composition. It still wasn't quite right. Maybe ze needed some more flowers. Or a different backdrop.

"Besides, I know you can handle this. It's just a cake tasting. You know what Alrik and I like. Why don't you just—"

"Yuuki," Hari said, interrupting whatever suggestion or excuse Yuuki had been about to make with what Katsuko called zir 'serious tone'. Hari loved zir cousin dearly, but there were some things ze just wasn't willing to do for him. Meeting with Darcie Alston, alone, was one of those things. "You're coming, or I'm cancelling. And if I cancel, we're marking it off the list, and you're picking from one of the one's we've already tried. That's the end of it. I'm not playing this game with you."

"I know you're not comfortable with her, but—"

"This isn't about comfortability." That was a lie, it was one hundred percent about the fact that Darcie Alston made Hari uncomfortable. But Hari knew that if Yuuki heard the lie in it, he wouldn't call zir on it. He was a good cousin like that. "This is about the fact that it's your wedding and you have to make the decision."

"What about if I send Alrik?"

"Yes, that's a brilliant plan. Send your confrontational fiancé to meet with the confrontational baker and your poor little soft spoken—"

"You're not soft spoken, don't fib." Yuuki laughed into the receiver. "But I see your point."

"I'm glad someone does. When I do that to Katsuko, she

just tunes me out." Hari muttered, turning to dig through the bin of fake flowers in the corner of zir office. Fresh flowers would have been better but ze hadn't had time to pick them up that morning, and this shoot needed to be done before ze headed out to meet with Yuuki. Especially since it was a paying gig.

"I might be a little late."

"So long as it's not more than ten minutes, I think we can make that work." Hari blew out a breath, rustling the long strands of hair from zir face. "I can deal with the awkwardness of her disdain for that long, I think."

"Disdain." Yuuki snorted, and Hari could just imagine him rolling his eyes. "As if anyone could feel that way about you."

"Yeah, surprised me too." Hari ignored the way the very thought made zir shoulders sag. Ze had never been able to deal with people not liking zir. Ze liked to be liked. Was that a crime?

"Okay then, I'll see you this afternoon."

"No more than ten minutes late. Promise?"

"Promise." Alrik said something in the background, muffled by the way Yuuki's shoulder held the phone to his ear. "I've got to go now. Love you!"

"Love you too." Hari tapped the end call button on zir phone and then slumped back into zir chair, letting it spin just a little. "A blanket! That's what this needs!" Ze hopped up from the chair to dig through the cupboard along the wall for a soft-colored throw.

FIFTEEN MINUTES. Yuuki was fifteen minutes late. Yuuki had never broken a promise before, especially not to

Hari. There had always been an understanding between them that they kept their promises. Ever since Hari's father had decided to take off and move to California, leaving zir mother, Katsuko, and Hari to have to move into that cramped apartment with Yuuki and his family, Yuuki had always kept his promises. And now . . .

And now he was twenty minutes late, according to Hari's phone.

Darcie sat across the table from Hari, her arms crossed over her chest, posture annoyed at being kept waiting. Not that Hari could blame her; people should keep their appointments. Especially when those people had promised Hari that they would. Ze was never going to let Yuuki live this down. Never.

"I'm sorry he's late," Hari said, forcing sincerity ze didn't quite feel into zir tone as ze checked zir phone for the fifth time. No text. No call. Nothing. Just late. "He and his fiancé run a food truck near the park, and tomorrow's their busy day, so they probably just got caught up with prepping."

"It's my busy day too," Darcie all but snapped. Which was severally unprofessional. Strike two.

"I'm aware." Hari took a breath and unclenched zir jaw. It wasn't Darcie's fault they were stuck here. It was Yuuki's, and likely Gwydion's. Still. "But since we have you for the hour, it's not like you didn't plan around this anyway."

"We'll have to rush the tasting."

"I'm sure that won't be a problem." The smile on Hari's face felt itchy and tight, like the moment when your mud mask dries and it's still not time to wash it off yet. But ze kept it there, because it was the only thing that was keeping zir from screaming. Or flinging zirself across the table, grabbing Darcie by her collar, and asking her why she didn't like Hari.

Ze was going to rip zir hair out. Yuuki would get there and find his cousin bald and hyperventilating and on the verge of—

"Sorry I'm late!" Yuuki wheezed out the words, pushing his hair back from his sweaty face. "We kept trying to close up shop, but people kept coming. And then I couldn't leave Alrik with all the prep for tomorrow, so I had to call Blaze to help. Which as you know is . . . Well, it's like trying to get a dragon to do anything." Yuuki let out a nervous laugh.

Hari rolled zir eyes but didn't say anything. It was hard to find anything funny at that moment, even a jab at Blaze.

"Hi. I'm Yuuki." Yuuki held out a hand for Darcie to shake, and she took it, a customer service smile pasted on her face. Hari resisted the urge to snort.

"Darcie Alston." Darcie gestured to the table, and Yuuki sat next to Hari, his shoulder pressing into zirs. "So, you two need a wedding cake. When are you getting married?"

Hari blinked for a moment, and then ze laughed, long and loud, throwing zir head back in perhaps the first real show of emotion ze had had since entering Gyeong's. Zir eyes burned, and zir lungs rasped around the sound.

Yuuki chuckled beside zir. "Oh. No. Hari's my cousin and . . . best person? Person of honor?"

"Wedding planner is more like it." Hari snorted when ze had caught zir breath again. "Yuuki's husband-to-be is named Alrik. I said earlier, they run a food truck."

Darcie had the audacity to look ashamed. "Right. You did. I'm sorry. I was . . . I've been distracted lately." She cleared her throat.

Yuuki shrugged it off. "At least Hari got a good laugh out of it."

Darcie nodded, her eyes drifting from Yuuki's to just over his shoulder. Hari had noticed that before, the woman didn't like making eye contact. Ze wondered if she was shy, or just nervous. It couldn't be nervous. She acted so sure of herself.

"Well. I'll go get the samples. I had Heather do them up this afternoon and put them in the fridge." Darcie rose from her chair and made a beeline for the back of the shop without giving Hari or Yuuki a chance to protest.

Hari saw Yuuki shift out of the corner of zir eye. "What is it?"

Yuuki shook his head, his nose scrunched up a little. "You said Darcie was the baker and owner, right? She'd inherited the place and the recipes from her mother and took over the business?"

"That's what their website says. I didn't exactly ask last time I was here. Remember, I got into a fight with her—"

"Then why does she have someone else preparing the samples for us?" Yuuki frowned, his fingers twisting in the loose-fitting mint-green shirt covered in cute tacos with faces.

"Maybe she was just cutting them, or plating them, or something." That was a reasonable assumption to make, Hari thought. There was no reason to jump to the conclusion that Darcie hadn't made the cakes herself. Yuuki didn't look placated, and Hari wasn't about to let whatever was going on with Darcie ruin Yuuki's special day. If zir cousin wanted the owner of this place to make his wedding cake, Hari would ensure that it happened. "Why don't we ask?"

"Oh. I don't want to offend her." Yuuki was getting himself worked up about it. Hari could see it. That was his way of things; he got himself spun up about things that ultimately didn't matter. He'd always been like that.

"I'll ask, to make sure," Hari said, a note of finality in zir tone.

Yuuki's shoulders relaxed, relief washing over his features like a wave. "Thank you, Haruki. You're the best."

"I am. And don't you forget it." Hari grinned, bumping zir shoulder against Yuuki's lightly and drawing a soft giggle from zir cousin. "There, that's better."

Darcie returned a minute later carrying a tray with different cakes and cups of icing on it. "We can mix and match most of the icings with the cakes. Just maybe not two of the berries, sometimes that gets a little too fruity, and then you wind up with something more like fruit punch than cake."

The tray was almost bigger than the table that Darcie set it on. She stood back, her hands clasped behind her back as Hari and Yuuki each took a fork and got to work trying the different cakes and icings. Occasionally Yuuki would ask about a flavor, but mostly they worked in silence. Hari could see Darcie rocking on her heels as ze and Yuuki carefully maneuvered samples around each other with the ease of two people who had known each other all their lives.

They had whittled it down to two cakes and two icings between them. Hari lifted zir head from the table to check with Yuuki.

Yuuki nodded.

Darcie cleared her throat looking severely uncomfortable with the silent communication between them, although Hari couldn't pinpoint why.

"So it looks like we want the purple yam with the cream cheese frosting as one tier, and the green tea with the chocolate frosting as another." Hari raised a brow at Yuuki, and Yuuki nodded again, before they both turned to Darcie.

"Is it . . . always like that with them?" Darcie asked someone over their shoulders, and they both turned to see

Alrik standing in the door, a laugh in his eyes. He was smiling That Smile at Yuuki, the one that had let Hari know that he was completely enamored. The one that made it obvious to anyone and everyone around them how Alrik felt about Yuuki.

"Always. Scary, right?" Alrik moved to the table, dragging a chair so he could press himself in close to Yuuki's other side. "Hey, save any for me?"

"You're not going to try to undo all the hard work we just put in agreeing with each other, are you?" Hari asked, eyes narrowed on where Alrik had moved to lean his head on Yuuki's shoulder and look up at him with puppy dog eyes.

"Me?" Alrik lifted his head, looking offended. "Would I do such a thing?"

"You would." Yuuki grinned, scooting their choices to Alrik and handing over his fork.

"No, I'm just here for the cake." Alrik leaned around Yuuki so he could grin at Hari and then shot Yuuki a wink before kissing his cheek.

"I think that's the first sensible thing I've ever heard you say." Hari huffed as Yuuki nudged zir foot under the table. Ze looked back to him, and Yuuki nodded at Darcie, and . . . oh, right. That's what they needed to talk about. "You said Heather made these? I was under the impression that everything that came out of Gyeong's was made by you. So she just prepared them?"

"No. She made them." Darcie shifted, her spine straightening more. "I have . . . decided to take a more hands-off approach to the bakery as of late. Heather is in charge of getting everything baked and out, while I step into a more managerial role."

"That won't do."

"What?" Darcie asked, and if Hari didn't know better, ze would have called that a squeak.

"I only want the best for my cousin. You've been making these recipes since you were a child. You're the best." Alrik and Yuuki had taken to scooping what was left of the samples up to feed to each other, Hari was pointedly ignoring their antics. "So, either you make the cake, or we go somewhere else."

"I—" Darcie took a deep breath, the motion making her collarbones stand out under her chef's jacket. "Heather makes them well enough, even if she's just a baker's assistant."

"But can she do so consistently, under the pressure of a wedding? Can she make the adjustments she'd need to make to create a stunning wedding cake for Yuuki and Alrik? You said she's not a baker. So she has no experience with these kinds of things. No. You'll make it, or we'll look somewhere else."

"I'm afraid that's impossible."

"Then we're going to have to think about it." Hari rose from zir seat and looked to the couple, who rose beside zir. "Thank you for time, Miss Alston."

"I don't really see where—"

"Thank you for your time." Hari felt the words like grit over zir tongue.

Ze didn't look back as ze made zir way to the door and out onto the street, the three of them walking side by side with Yuuki in the middle. Hari could see Yuuki's face doing something out of the corner of zir eye, but ze wasn't sure what exactly. Still, it was easy to guess.

"Don't give me that look." Hari sighed.

"What look?" Yuuki looked up at zir innocently.

"You've made up your mind, haven't you?"

Yuuki shrugged.

"It was the purple yam, wasn't it?"

Another shrug.

"I hate you, you know that?"

"That's a lie."

"What if I can't get her to agree to make it for you?" Hari didn't really think that was a problem; ze had a knack for getting people to do things. Although Darcie Alston seemed . . . more difficult.

"Oh, I wouldn't worry about that. You're very charming."

"Flattery, dear cousin, will get you everywhere."

"I know." Yuuki grinned brightly, bouncing on his toes as he walked.

"Fine. I'll email her in the morning to place your order. Any other miracles you'd like me to work for this wedding? Perhaps you'd like flying pigs released instead of doves?"

"I don't think that'd be very sanitary, Hari." Yuuki grinned cheekily, and Alrik choked on a laugh.

"You owe me big for this. Both of you."

"Hey. Why am I being included in this?" Alrik huffed.

"Because you're marrying him. That's why."

Yuuki grabbed Hari's wrist and pulled zir to a stop in the middle of the sidewalk, then bounced up to kiss zir cheek. "You're the best, Hari. Has anyone ever told you that?"

"Frequently."

And then they were all laughing, and Hari felt the tension from zir encounter with Darcie dissipate entirely.

SEVEN

She wasn't going to see Lily; Darcie had made up her mind about that. She was not going to go down the block to Stargazer's and confront Lily about moving in on Gyeong's territory. It wouldn't do anyone any good. All it would do was make her feel worse. It would drag up old hurts. It would—

Someone knocked on the door to Darcie's office. She looked up to see Sarah smiling sheepishly. "The person who ordered the wedding cake is here."

"Why? We don't have an appointment for another month, at least, to go over decorations." But Darcie was already up from her seat, following Sarah out the door and into the front of the bakery. Hari was there, as Sarah had said. Ze had dragged zir table to the window again. Zir blue hair was tied back in a messy bun, strands falling into zir face as ze bent over a kkwabaegi with zir phone.

Sarah shrugged, stopping at the counter to tidy something that didn't really look like it needed tidying. Darcie shook her head and made her way over to Hari.

"We don't have an appointment," she said again. Which

she realized was silly. If Hari wanted to show up and waste zir time at Gyeong's, ze was more than allowed to. Still, it seemed strange. Darcie hadn't exactly been welcoming.

Hari looked up to fix Darcie with that glaring smile again, rivaling the summer sunshine that reflected off the cars outside. "No, we don't."

Darcie pressed her lips tightly to keep herself from saying something stupid. That seemed to be her go-to with Hari: look at zir blinding smile and say something stupid. She wasn't exactly sure why. Her filter between her brain and her mouth usually worked so much better than that.

"But I was craving a mochi bun, and then I got here and the kkwabaegi looked so good. So." Hari shrugged, turning back to the picture ze'd been arranging. Ze had been right, the lighting by the window was better. And even with the brown paper bag on the brown table, it helped to highlight the crispy golden crust of the elegantly twisted donut.

"Your pictures are nice," Darcie heard herself say, though she wasn't sure when she had told her mouth it was allowed to speak. In fact, she was pretty sure she'd told it it wasn't.

Hari looked up again, zir dark eyes widened a little.

"The ones on your blog, they're nice." She sounded ridiculous. She sounded inarticulate. She sounded like she was speaking nothing but drivel. Why was she like this?

"Oh. Thanks!" Hari brightened, zir nose wrinkling a little with the new smile. "I mean, like I said, I think it'd be great if you had some kind of branding on your bags. Something to tell people that the pastries were from Gyeong's. It doesn't even have to have the name. Just a symbol."

Darcie opened her mouth to argue. To tell Hari that that was a stupid idea. But then she thought back to the lily stamped onto the white sack. "I'll think about it."

"Really?"

Darcie nodded, chewing on the inside of her cheek to keep from saying anything else foolish.

"Good. That's good." Hari ducked back to zir work, taking another series of shots before taking a bite from the donut and murmuring softly.

Darcie should leave. She should walk away and let Hari enjoy zir kkwabaegi. But even as she thought the words, she couldn't get her body to cooperate and move. It was like Hari was some kind of magnet, a riptide, pulling her in and keeping her there. Ugh. When had she become so poetic? Gross. That was gross.

"Did you have any other suggestions?" No. No, no. She most certainly hadn't given her mouth permission to say *that*.

Hari's head jerked again, dark brows disappearing into the shadow of zir hat. "Really?"

Darcie's head nodded, again, without her permission. What was going on with her today? It was the lack of sleep. It was the concern over the bakery. It was Gwydion's curse.

"I'd start with your lights." Hari pointed up to the black pendant lights hanging from the ceiling. "Natural light is best, but there's only so much of that you can get in a space like this. So the next best thing is good bulbs. You've got some really hard incandescent bulbs up there. They're making this place feel more like an interrogation room in a bad cop movie than a bakery."

"What?" Darcie looked up at the lights, blinking when the glare from them burned her eyes.

"You want something softer for a space like this. Less direct but still bright. They're more expensive, but LED bulbs would provide the kind of light you want."

Darcie nodded dumbly.

"I mean, ideally, you'd want to replace those horrible pendant lights. They're doing nothing for this space, but that's more of an ordeal than just swapping out the bulbs."

"Replace the lights?"

Hari smiled a little, grabbing zir phone to pull up a browser and do a quick search. When ze had found what ze was looking for, ze held it up for Darcie to see. "Track lighting is really the best option. This is what I have in my place. It lets you direct the light to where it's needed. To fill in gaps, so you get a more overall lit room instead of these . . . " Hari gestured to where, Darcie was just now realizing, a hard beam of light landed on a table in the middle of the bakery, leaving the area around it in darkness. "Ambient light is best."

"Right." Darcie wasn't sure what that meant. She'd have to do a search after Hari left. "Why do you know so much about light bulbs?"

Hari blinked and then let out a low, self-deprecating chuckle. "You pick things up when you get into photography. Lighting is kind of the most important part."

"It is?" *Oh, and we're back to inarticulate, bumbling fool. Good. Because this interaction wasn't awkward enough.* Darcie bit hard at the side of her tongue to keep any more idiocy from coming out of her mouth.

"Well, yeah." Hari rubbed at the tip of zir nose as if it itched. "You can make almost anything look good if you have the proper lighting. You could also raise the lights up a bit, so they cast a wider, softer beam. But I'd start with the bulbs themselves, see where that gets you. It doesn't require going up into the ceiling."

"I'll have to try that."

Hari looked back down at zir phone, zir fingers tapping

nervously against the screen. "I can . . . I can send you some links to the bulbs I use at my place."

"I would appreciate that."

Hari took a breath, seeming to gather zirself, and then held zir phone out to Darcie. "Put in your number, and I'll send you some links."

Darcie tightened her jaw to keep it from falling slack and took the phone to type in her number. Then she promptly handed it back, bunny phone case and all. "Thank you. For your assistance."

"Sure! That's what friends do, right?" Hari's smile was sunny again, zir head tilting to one side. "I'll send them over later, okay? I've got an appointment to get to."

Darcie nodded.

"Great." Hari stood, slinging zir messenger bag over zir shoulder and grabbing zir donut. "Talk to you later."

Ze was out the door before Darcie could even raise her hand to wave goodbye, and she was left standing there, watching Hari disappear down the street.

ANOTHER DAY, another crappy review. It wasn't that Heather wasn't a good baker—she was—she just didn't have it in her blood the way Darcie did. Or maybe it was less that and more the reviews from when Darcie had been handling the baking. The ones that had been left because of Gwydion's curse. It hadn't been long, just over a week, but it had been enough to turn the tide of Gyeong's reputation.

Darcie slumped forward at her desk, pressing her forehead into the cool wood surface, only just barely missing the keyboard. There was nothing that could be done about bad reviews, she reminded herself. All she could hope was to get some good ones that would bury the bad. Which would mean *getting* good reviews. Which would mean . . . doing *something* to *get* good reviews? But . . . what?

Her phone dinged with a notification, and she groaned loudly, hoping it wasn't another review. Lifting her head, she only just caught the little message symbol before the screen darkened again. She tapped at the glass and squinted down at the bubble on the screen. It was definitely a text, from an unknown number. Sitting up, she read the message preview, wrinkling her nose.

Unknown Number: You looked sad today
    Here's a picture of my bunnies
    / (^ × ^) \

THERE WAS AN IMAGE ATTACHMENT. She was pretty sure she shouldn't open a text that claimed to have "bunnies" in it and had an image attached. She glared down at the unknown number, trying to parse out if she'd ever seen it before, but nothing came to mind.

Unknown Number: Oh! BTW
    (o ′ ▽ ` o) / It's Hari!

Darcie rolled her eyes, letting out a breath. Hari. Of course it was Hari. Who else would randomly send her pictures of bunnies? She opened the text and couldn't help the smile that tugged at her cheeks. In the picture there were two fluffy, lop-eared rabbits. One black. One White. Both were contentedly chewing on what looked like parsley.

Unknown Number: ZhanZhan and YingYing say hi!

I hope I'm not bothering you

You never said if you liked rabbits or not. I'm just making the assumption that you do. Because only psychopaths don't like bunnies.

You're not a psychopath, are you Darcie?

Darcie blinked for a moment at the screen, her eyes widening at the rapid succession of texts. She didn't know what she'd been expecting when Hari texted her, but she supposed she should have known ze'd text just the way ze talked.

It took her a moment to realize she hadn't texted back, and then she let out a breath and typed.

Darcie: Not that I'm aware of.

The little dots popped up to let her know that Hari was typing back, blinking in rapid succession, and then ze seemed to stop, maybe backspacing? Darcie moved to add zir number to her contact list while she waited. At least then she wouldn't have to continue to look at the long string of numbers which was honestly giving her a headache. She set the picture as the picture of ZhanZhan and YingYing and was just about to text something else when Hari responded.

Hari: . . . . . .

Was that a joke?

Darcie . . .

Are you funny?

Why didn't you tell me you were funny?!

Darcie snorted, her fingers tapping against the screen, trying to think of a pithy come back. She wasn't sure why it mattered if it were pithy or not, but she found herself wanting to impress Hari. Wanting to make zir smile. And it was so much easier to do that via text than it ever would be in person.

Darcie: I don't like to advertise it.

She wrinkled her nose. That wasn't pithy. That wasn't even remotely funny. Granted, she hadn't expected her assurances that she wasn't a psychopath to be funny either. Before she could type anything else, she got another message from Hari.

Hari: Well that's a shame ヾ(￣O￣)ツ
    Darcie: Why?

She wasn't sure she actually wanted to know why. But the word had slipped from her fingers onto the keys, and it was sent before she could think better of it.

Hari: ¯\(″ᵕ‵″)/¯
    I like funny people
    Darcie: Oh.

Oh? Oh?! *Oh*?! Is that the best she could do? Was oh?! Darcie dropped her head back to the desk, smacking it against the table again. Why was she like this?

The little dots appeared again. Then disappeared. Then appeared. Then disappeared. And Darcie found herself holding her breath, hoping she hadn't just scared Hari off with her complete and utter ineptitude. Seriously, why had she thought texting with zir would be easier than talking in person?

> Hari: Well
>> Anyway
>> I just wanted to send you the link to the lightbulbs

And there was a link attached below those words. When Darcie clicked it, it brought her to a webpage hosting different sized LED bulbs. Closing out of it, she went back to their chat window.

> Darcie: Thank you.
>> Hari: Of course!
>> <(‾ ‿ ‾)>
>> Let me know if there is anything else I can do
>> I'm always happy to talk shop!

Darcie resisted the urge to ask why. Asking why would jinx it. Hari would rethink the help ze was offering, and it would turn into a *thing*. Besides, she didn't need help, did she? She was doing just fine on her own. In spite of the reviews and the lowered sales. All of that could be chalked up to summer vacation ending and a little bad press. Nothing Gyeong's couldn't bounce back from. Nothing they hadn't bounced back from before. She'd be fine.

> Darcie: I'll let you know if I have any other questions. Thank you.
>> Hari: (~˘▼˘)~ anytime

Darcie bit her lip, looking down at the most recent text,

and let out another long breath. It wasn't a good idea, she told herself, even as her fingers flew across the screen.

> Darcie: Please stop by the bakery tomorrow. I would like
> to thank you for your assistance in person.

And then she put her phone on silent, tucked it into the desk drawer, and went back to the kitchen. It wasn't a good idea, but she was going to do it anyways, because Hari's bunnies were very cute.

That was the only reason.

She gathered up the ingredients for a mochi bun dough and got started. She wasn't even sure if this dough would work as bunny shapes, but she could try.

EIGHT

"I didn't think you liked the baker," said a voice over zir shoulder. It was close enough to zir ear that Hari could tell Gwydion had leaned over the back of the couch to read zir text messages.

"How did you get in here?" Hari locked zir phone and dropped it into zir lap, away from prying eyes.

Gwydion's mouth tugged up into a smirk as they moved to settle down onto the sofa beside Hari. "Magic. Now, the baker?"

"That's breaking and entering." Hari wasn't exactly sure why ze felt so disgruntled at having Gwydion in zir space all of a sudden. Likely because of the conversation between ze and Darcie. It had been . . . well, it had been rather nice. There was a part of Hari, however small, that always felt like ze was giving something of zirself up to make sure people liked zir. This hadn't felt like that. Although, Hari couldn't explain why.

"There was no breaking involved. And is it really entering if I just kind appeared in the middle of your living room?" Gwydion tilted their head to one side, long red hair falling over their shoulder into their face in perfect waves. They must use magic to achieve that look, Hari decided. There was no other earthly way it could work.

Hari raised a brow, lips pursed in mild annoyance. Not just at Gwydion's unsubtly perfectly magicked hair, but at the fact that Gwydion was there at all.

Gwydion laughed and winked. "Besides, I'm like a vampire. Once you invite me in, I've got free rein over your life. Maybe Alrik should have warned you about that."

"He definitely should have." Hari's phone buzzed again, but ze left it turned over in zir lap. It was Darcie, ze knew it was. But Hari wasn't about to have a conversation with Darcie while Gwydion looked over zir shoulder. Maybe there was something to Blaze's annoyance with the witch after all. They did seem to like to meddle.

"Aren't you going to get that?"

"Why are you here, Gwydion?" It was unusually sharp, Hari knew that. Ze wasn't normally so irritable. But there seemed to be something private about the side of herself that Darcie was revealing to Hari. Something ze knew Darcie wouldn't want anyone else to see, especially not the witch who had cursed her.

"Can't I just stop in and say hello to a friend?"

Hari's eye twitched. Ze wondered how frequently Gwydion played the game of answering a question with a question. They seemed terribly well practiced. "Gwydion."

Gwydion chuckled, twisting their body to lean against the arm of the couch so they could look at Hari properly. Hari's phone buzzed again, a reminder that ze had a text still unread. Ze hoped Darcie wasn't waiting for an immediate answer. Either way, the alert was giving Hari anxiety. Ze could feel the need to look at it like a physical drag under zir skin. Ze had never gone so long without answering a text unless zir phone was somewhere out of reach.

"What're you here for?" Hari tried again, ignoring the way zir jaw tightened around the words. It wouldn't do to make the witch angry, ze knew that. Ze had seen enough of what Gwydion was capable of. Still, Hari had to know, how far did Gwydion's reach extend? Were they doing something to make Darcie somehow more amiable? That didn't seem fair.

"I just wanted to check in about the wedding plans and see if you needed any help." Gwydion shrugged. "I've planned a fair few weddings in my day. Although the last was . . . Well, it's been a couple hundred years or so."

"I think Katsuko and I have it covered. I'll let you know if I need anything though."

"All right then." Gwydion's grin turned into a smirk, their head tilting again in question. "How are negotiations with the baker going?"

Hari let out a breath, letting zir shoulders sink deeper into the plush cushions of the couch. ZhanZhan looked up from his hutch as if worried but didn't move to leave it. Ying-Ying slept soundly beside him. "Better."

"She still hasn't agreed to make the cake herself."

"No. Are you going to tell me what her curse is?"

Gwydion hummed, lips pursed together, and then they shook their head. "No. I don't think so. I think she should tell you. Or maybe you'll just find out on your own. Either way, she needs to put on her big girl pants and ask for help if she wants it."

"She's been getting a lot of negative feedback on the bakery as of late." Hari scrubbed at zir undercut. It would be better to just have this conversation, then maybe Gwydion would go away, and ze would finally be able to look at zir texts.

"Mhm."

"And add to that the new place down the block, which is arguably adorable. They even have a 'grammable wall set up for selfies. It's perfect."

"Stargazer's. Yes, I've seen it."

"Although nothing they make is half as good as Gyeong's."

"No, of course not. Darcie Alston loves baking. She's been doing it since she was old enough to walk."

Hari blinked at Gwydion and wondered why they were telling zir this. Why they were having this conversation with zir at all. "Then why has she given it up?"

Gwydion gave a dainty shrug. "Another thing you'll have to ask her, I suppose. Anyway, I was just checking in on the wedding plans. I didn't mean to get so caught up talking about one of my charges."

"Of course you didn't." Hari eyed the witch through narrowed eyes. Ze wasn't fooled. Maybe the others were, but not Hari. Hari had been using dramatics and glitter to hide behind since ze was a teenager. Ze could smell it on someone else a mile away. "You're lonely, aren't you?"

Gwydion rose from the couch and headed for the door. "Tell Yuuki and Alrik that I'm here if they need a hand with things. And let Blaze know that his dog peed in my shoe when he was last at my place, and I know it was under orders from him. So he owes me a new pair of pumps."

Then they were gone, disappearing before they even reached the door down the hall. Hari sighed, rolling zir eyes. Ze supposed ze shouldn't have expected a straight answer when Hari hadn't given Gwydion one either.

Shaking zir head, Hari looked down at zir phone finally.

A little smile twitched at the corner of Hari's lips. It was from Darcie. An invitation. To be thanked in person. Maybe Darcie was warming up to zir after all.

HARI WASN'T sure what ze had been expecting when ze'd woken up "extra early" that morning—which was sleeping in for most people, Darcie Alston included. But whatever it had been, it hadn't been to find two adorably crafted bunny mochi buns staring back at zir from atop pastry bags. Darcie had even used a little food dye to make one of them look almost black. Well, more gray than anything else, but the effort was there, and it was sweet.

"Did you make these?" Hari's eyes flicked from the buns up to Darcie who was standing behind the counter with her hands tucked behind her back. Hari wondered if she was fidgeting.

"Yes, there is a whole batch if you'd like them. I couldn't make just two, the recipe doesn't allow for that. But . . . "

"Oh no! Put them in the case! Make them a special of the day. You can't share this adorableness with just me." Hari laughed brightly. "Besides, I can't possibly eat a whole batch by myself, and they shouldn't go to waste."

"I made them for you," Darcie said plainly. She almost sounded a little offended about the idea of selling the bunny buns.

Hari tilted zir head, loose hair falling into zir face. Ze should have tied it back this morning, but honestly, there had been no time. It was brush hair and do make up or go plain faced and do hair. The second wasn't really an option, not in Hari's opinion.

"And they're wonderful." Hari brushed the hair back

from zir face, still grinning. "They're honestly the cutest thing I've ever seen, and I am one hundred percent going to take tons of pictures of them, and post them everywhere, and tell everyone to come here and pick up the rest. Honestly, you'll probably have a line out the door again."

"But?"

"But they made me smile, and they should have a chance to make other people smile too. Don't you think?"

Darcie opened her mouth as if to argue, her eyes had gone impossibly wide. And then she let out a breath and just nodded. "Will you at least try them before I do that? I've had . . . I've had some problems lately with the flavors on things."

"Of course! But only if you promise I can have a third for pictures."

Darcie nodded, already reaching for another pastry bag to put another bunny bun into it as Hari grabbed up the white one and tore off a bite with zir teeth. The flavor settled in layers over zir tongue as ze chewed, drawing a happy murmur. First doughy, then the sesame seeds, then a faint buttery taste, warm and smooth on the palette.

"These are really good! You said you've had problems with your favors lately?" Hari asked around a second mouthful. "What's been the problem?"

Darcie shrugged awkwardly, sliding the other bun over the counter to Hari. "Will you send me the pictures?"

"Of course! And I'm going to post them on my accounts, so you better make up a sign for them." Hari watched Darcie let out another breath and nod. She didn't seem as sad as she had the previous day. Nor as stressed, really. It was like making something had set her free. Even if there were bags under her eyes. "Darcie . . . can I ask you something?"

"I'd really rather you didn't." Darcie frowned down at her feet.

Hari sighed and nodded. Ze should have known that would be the answer. Ze wasn't sure why ze'd expected anything else. It wasn't like they were friends. At least not yet. But Hari could see it. They were getting there. They might be if ze just tried a little harder. This wasn't about being liked, as Katsuko might imply. No, this was about the fact that Darcie needed a friend, and Hari . . . Well, Hari was just good at getting people to open up, all right?

"We won't talk about that then," Hari promised. Ze wasn't sure if Darcie knew ze meant the curse or not, but it didn't really matter. Hari wouldn't bring it up until she did. "But you look like you could use a break. Why don't we go get lunch?"

Darcie looked up from her shoes to blink at Hari. Her dark eyes widened just enough that Hari noticed but not enough that anyone further away was likely to. Her gaze flicked around Hari's face, searching for . . . something. Hari wasn't sure what. Then Darcie was looking over zir shoulder, not making eye contact again.

"I can't leave the bakery. But thank you for the offer."

The girl behind the register, not even a foot away, looked between them. Looked at the empty dining area. Looked between them again. Then let out a little huff before turning back to fiddling with whatever she'd been working on on her phone. Hari had half expected her to argue, but it would seem no one wanted to argue with Darcie. Probably because she'd win. She seemed the type.

"Then I'll bring something back, and we can eat here. What are you feeling? Burgers? Salads? Burritos? I could even head uptown to Yuuki and Alrik's food truck. Yuuki makes the best ramen. I just need to know if you have any dietary restrictions. Like . . . are you vegan? No. That's silly. If you were vegan, you'd have a vegan bakery, wouldn't you?"

Darcie blinked, her eyes settling back on Hari as ze talked a mile a minute. She seemed . . . overwhelmed? Confused? Lost? No. Her mouth twitched a little, just the slightest, at the corner. She was amused. Oh. That was a good look on her.

"A burrito would be good."

"Great! Just text me your order and I'll pick it up. I know a place a couple blocks over. They make the best burritos in this part of the city. I'll be back soon. Yeah?"

Darcie nodded.

NINE

Hari came back forty-five minutes later, paper bag in hand and a wide smile on zir face. Darcie hadn't actually thought ze would come back, although she wasn't sure why.

"I'll take some pictures after we eat and help you make up that sign, all right?" Hari dropped into zir table, the one by the window that Darcie hadn't moved back yet. Ze took out a tin foil wrapped loaf and sat it across from zir on the table, then gave the top a tap. An invitation.

Darcie blinked, her eyes flicking back to Sarah, who stood behind the register. Sarah rolled her eyes and gave a tiny nod before going back to pretending she wasn't paying attention to Hari's antics at all.

"Come on then. You'll need your strength for all the customers you're about to get," Hari said with all the confidence of someone who had never met a person ze didn't like.

"Don't talk with your mouth full," Darcie scolded, but made her way around the glass case to sit across from Hari anyway. Her words sent Hari into a delighted giggle that only ended when ze started coughing because zir food had gone down the wrong way. "This is why you shouldn't talk while eating."

"Right. Right. Yes ma'am." Hari gave a lazy salute and went back to her own burrito.

The quiet that stretched between them only lasted as long as it took Darcie to unwrap her lunch. And then Hari was leaning forward on the table, zir elbows digging into the wood. "Did you have a chance to look at the light bulbs I sent you?"

Darcie took a bite from her food, chewed slowly, and ignored the pained look on Hari's face as ze waited in suspense for her to chew and swallow. It was actually quite fun to watch zir squirm, but Darcie tried to not find too much twisted amusement in it. That would be cruel. When she was done, she set the burrito down on the tin foil again and looked up.

"I ordered a pack of those bulbs to try in our lights. I have also set aside time this weekend to raise the pendant lights, per your suggestion." The lights needed to be dusted anyway, it wouldn't be too hard to do that at the same time. Or at least she hoped not. She'd never been up into the ceiling before to see what was up there. That had always been Appa's job. And then after he'd passed . . . Well, no one else had ever bothered to go up there. Thankfully, they'd never had any issues that required it.

"Good! Good! I could come by and help if you'd like. I'm not an electrician or anything, but I put up the track lighting in my place without electrocuting myself."

"Truly impressive."

Hari threw zir head back with the kind of laugh that could wake the dead. Darcie looked wide eyed from Hari to Sarah behind the counter, who was ignoring them entirely in favor of doing something on her phone, and back. It took Hari a minute to wind down, and when ze did, ze wiped at the corners of zir eyes as if ze had been crying.

"You need to warn me next time you decide to be funny, Darcie. I could have choked and died."

Darcie blushed hotly, grateful her neck and ears were hidden by the shoulder-length bob of dark hair. She didn't think she'd survive the embarrassment if Hari realized how zir compliments affected her.

"Eat your lunch. We have things to do," she said to cover the way she shifted in her seat.

"Aye aye, cap'n." Hari saluted again and then dug into zir lunch.

When they were done, Hari set to work taking a series of shots of the bunny buns that could easily have gone in a food magazine, in Darcie's humble opinion. And then ze drew up a sign for the front door to lure people in. It had a little rabbit on it, which was arguably adorable.

"Text me and let me know how it goes," Hari called over zir shoulder by way of goodbye when it was all done. The bell tinkled above the door to let everyone know ze had departed.

Sarah was staring at Darcie, her gaze practically boring a hole into Darcie's cheek. "We're not talking about that."

"Didn't think so," Sarah said, but there was a knowing smile on her lips that said she didn't need to talk about it. She'd apparently seen enough to draw her own conclusions.

"I'm going to check on Heather in the back. Let me know if we sell any of them." Darcie heard Sarah hum an agreement just before the door to the kitchen swung shut behind her.

THEY SOLD out in under two hours. And that was how it started. From there, Darcie couldn't seem to stop the flood of texts, or the frequent visits with lunch, although to be perfectly frank, she wasn't sure that she'd even tried more than half-heartedly. They talked every day, and it was just . . . it was so easy. Even when Darcie didn't feel like she had a lot to say, Hari seemed perfectly content to fill the silence.

Their conversations ranged from ways to improve Gyeong's to the new restaurant that Hari had just tried. It was . . . it was nice. And with Hari's added attention, things at Gyeong's were getting better. Darcie still didn't feel comfortable baking for the shop, but people were coming in, and sales were up. It was almost funny how a handful of small changes could make such a big difference.

"You know, I never asked," Hari started one day a couple of weeks later, zir chopsticks stopped mid-air where they held a piece of sushi, zir brows pressed together in thought.

Darcie looked up from her own plate to eye the suddenly serious press of Hari's lips. She let out a breath, setting down her chopsticks on the plate and folding her hands into her lap. "Never asked what?"

"Why did you stop baking?"

She felt her shoulders sag. For some reason, she had thought they had come to an agreement not to talk about this. Or maybe it had been something else Hari had said ze wouldn't ask about. Darcie shrugged that thought aside. It didn't matter. None of it mattered. Because now Hari had asked, and Darcie would have to either avoid the question entirely, lie, or—

"You don't have to answer if it makes you uncomfortable," Hari said, breaking that train of thought. "I understand that sometimes these choices are personal, and if yours is, then that's okay."

"What?" Darcie fingers tightened in her lap. People didn't do that, right? Usually, they wanted an answer. All of her other friends would have wanted an answer. Lily had wanted one when Darcie had decided not to go to Paris with her. Why didn't Hari demand an answer?

"If you aren't ready to tell me, then you're not ready to tell me. I'm not going to force you just to satiate my curiosity." Hari scrubbed at the tip of zir nose. "It's not fair to do that."

"Thank you," Darcie said on a breath, her hands relaxing in her lap. She took up her chopsticks again, taking a measured bite to buy herself time. For what? She wasn't sure. Maybe just to feel normal again, instead of feeling so overwhelmed by the sincerity of that statement. It had settled like a weight in her chest, and Darcie didn't know what to do with it.

"No problem." Hari nodded, humming happily, and took the bite that had been hanging from zir chopsticks. "So what're you doing this weekend?"

And then it was over, whatever tension had been between them melted away. Which was weird in and of itself. Darcie had never been in a situation before where she'd made things awkward and the other person had promptly shrugged it off and moved on with life. Usually people sat with the awkward, tried to stretch it out because they didn't know what to say. Or perhaps they wanted to punish her for making things weird. Hari . . . Hari wasn't like that.

"Working." Even as she said the word, Darcie felt the boring tone, the flat voice the . . . everything that Hari was not.

Hari laughed, zir head tilted to let a long lock of dark purple hair fall into zir face. Ze'd re-dyed it last week, and

Darcie had yet to have the heart to tell zir that she'd liked it better blue. "Well, obviously. But in the evenings, I mean. That's not all you do, right? You don't just work at the bakery. I mean, it's not even open that late on the weekends, so of course you don't."

"There is the accounting, and the ordering, and payroll. There is always something to do."

"Fine. Fine." Hari waved zir hand through the air, chopsticks still clutched between zir fingers. "Take a night off from all that. I'm sure you're at least a month ahead on it, if not more."

"And do what?"

"Come to my place." Hari picked up a gyoza from the tray in the middle of the table, stuffing the whole thing into zir mouth before grinning wildly at Darcie. "You need to come meet ZhanZhan and YingYing."

"I do?"

"Of course you do! They inspired your best-selling bunny buns. Don't they deserve a little credit? We'll get takeout and cuddle the bunnies. I'd offer to cook, but last time I tried, Alrik accused me of trying to kill him so . . ."

"Don't you have something else you'd rather do than hang out with me all night?"

Hari blinked for a minute and then snorted. "Of course not. Come on, it'll be fun, I promise. We can watch bad movies, and eat popcorn, and give ZhanZhan all the cuddles he wants. Because, let's face it, ZhanZhan is an attention hog. What do you say?"

"All right," Darcie said, before she could think better of it. Because she was sure she would think better of it. If she let herself dwell in the possibilities of what this was or was not, she most definitely would think better of it. She'd tell

Hari no, and she'd just spend her night running the numbers, like she did every weekend.

"Saturday. I'll pick you up here after the bakery closes. Is that okay?"

"I should meet you at your place. There'll be things to do here after close. I have to clean up the kitchen, check the inventory, lock up the—"

"If I let you meet me at my place, how likely are you to just text and back out? On a scale of one to ten." Hari leaned back in zir seat, that knowing smirk on zir lips.

Darcie hated that smirk, but she couldn't deny Hari was probably right. If ze didn't pick her up, she would probably back out last minute. Maybe not lie, but maybe say she wasn't feeling up to it. It wasn't that she didn't want to go, it was that after a full day of "peopling," she may not have it in her for more. What felt like a good idea now may not feel like one come Saturday. She'd also probably work herself up into a frenzy about the undercurrent of implications, and all the things that could go wrong, and all the stupid things she'd said prior to the invitation that were no doubt echoing in Hari's brain.

"You're spiraling," Hari said, drawing her back to their little table in front of the window. "And this is how I know that if I don't pick you up, you'll bail."

"I will not." Darcie lifted her chin, feeling suddenly defensive.

Hari raised a brow.

"All right." Her shoulders slumped. "You can pick me up."

"Perfect!" Hari clapped, sending the sushi between zir chopsticks flying with a yelp. "Oh! Sorry! Sorry! My bad!" Ze jumped up with a napkin to clean up the sauce left behind on the floor.

TEN

Saturday had been a mess. A complete and utter mess. YingYing had hidden under the bed and refused to come out. The "simple" cupcake recipe Yuuki had written up had turned out to be anything but. Hari's place was a disaster zone, and ZhanZhan had decided to sit in the middle of the living room and not move for the entire hour ze tried to vacuum around him. Add to all that that zir client had been late and hadn't brought anything by way of ideas or samples so Hari could start on the work, and Hari was one stressed out human.

Still, ze had a night planned with Darcie, and ze was not about to reschedule. It had been too difficult to get Darcie to agree to the date to begin with, and to gather the courage to ask her. Well, maybe "date" wasn't the right word. But Hari didn't have a better one to describe what ze had planned, so ze had been calling it a date all week. Secretly. In zir head. Mainly because Yuuki and Katsuko were already having a field day with the idea of Hari going on a date with Darcie. No need to confirm their assumptions.

"You can't just *buy* cupcakes to replace the ones you

were going to make for a *baker*." Hari heard a soft thump on the other side of the phone and could imagine Aura banging her head on the wall, or desk, or counter, or table, or whatever was in the closest vicinity to bang her head against. "Eero, tell zir."

"I'm not getting in the middle of this. The last time I tried to give dating advice, Blaze almost set my hair on fire." Eero was farther away from the phone, likely on the couch or in the kitchen.

"Well, Hari isn't a dragon, so I doubt ze is going to set your hair on fire. You're not going to set his hair on fire, are you?" Aura sounded like she was rolling her eyes. Hari wasn't sure how ze knew, it was just a tone of voice.

"Ze still could! It's called a lighter, Aura. I might not be as young and hip as you two—"

Aura scoffed. Another eye roll, very likely.

"—but I know how lighters work!"

"I always forget that you're an old man. How old are you, again?" Aura's voice warbled a little with laughter.

Honestly, Hari wasn't even sure why ze'd bothered calling them. Ze knew ze wouldn't be able to get a word in edgewise between the two of them. Not if they were together. Because they'd spend the entire time flirting. Which was so unproductive to Hari's plight, it wasn't even funny. But it had felt nice to vent, for the whole five minutes they'd allowed zir to.

Eero mumbled something.

Hari couldn't ever be sure exactly how old the fairy was, but ze knew that Eero and Blaze had been on the Titanic together. So that was some indication.

"What was that? You're going to have to speak up."

"Old enough!" Eero huffed.

"Old enough for what?"

"All right, this is all very cute and all. But will you two stop flirting long enough to help me with my problem?" Hari asked. "Preferably before I have to get on the subway and head down to K-town to pick her up."

"We weren't flirting." Eero's voice was louder. He'd likely moved to sit next to Aura. Hari was grateful that they both seemed to finally be focusing.

"I thought we solved your problem. You can't give a baker grocery store cupcakes. Those are the rules." Aura's fingernails tapped against the table impatiently.

"Where are these rules written? Is there a book of them I need to see? What's it called?" Hari couldn't help the smile that slipped onto zir lips. It was easy to forget the utter disaster this date was probably going to be in the face of zir friends being silly.

"It's called Hari Atsushi Gets Some Common Sense. It's a picture book, you'll like it."

Eero choked on a laugh in the background.

"Does it also feature tips on how to get that fairy you're covertly dating to realize it? *Oh*! Or maybe it'll have a how-to guide on telling your quote, unquote 'good friend' that you're not really dating that pixie, and—"

"Hanging up now," Aura announced through what sounded like clenched teeth, and if Hari were a betting person, blushing cheeks.

"Good luck on your date, Hari!" Eero called.

And then the line went silent, and Hari pulled zir phone away from zir ear, laughing softly. "They'll get it together eventually," ze said, typing out a quick text to the group chat.

Hari: RUDE!

No answer came before ze reached the subway, and honestly, that was probably for the best. It wasn't like they could really give any advice, not seeing how messed up their own . . . whatever was. Hari shook zir head, stuffing zir phone in zir pocket. Ze would just have to figure it out on zir own.

And ze was going to, honestly, but the ride on the subway yielded no results. Nor did the walk from the platform to the bakery. And by the time Hari reached the front door of Gyeong's, ze was more sure than ever that this date was a disaster waiting to happen. Seriously, it was going to blow up in zir face.

Hari's phone buzzed in zir pocket, and ze laughed at the message from Yuuki.

Yuuki: Fighting! (๑•̀ㅂ•́)و

The bakery was quiet but for the soft chime of the bell above the door.

One of the girls was putting up the chairs, and she smiled when she saw Hari. "Darcie's in the kitchen, checking the inventory. You can head right back. I'll lock the door on my way out."

"Thanks. How was today?" Hari moved to help her finish stacking the chairs.

"It seems like we did okay, but boss would be able to tell you better than me. She's in a good mood, at least."

"Good. I'm glad." Hari stood back from where ze had finished putting up the chairs, arms swaying at zir sides against zir long skirt. Ze had spent hours trying on different things in zir closet to find the perfect outfit. It wasn't like Hari was nervous or that going on a date was unusual. It was just that . . . Well, ze wanted to make a good impression. That was all.

"I think she's excited about your date."

"It's not a—"

"Right. Of course it isn't." She winked. "I'll see you tomorrow?"

"Yeah . . . probably."

"Good." She nodded and headed out the door, locking it behind her.

Hari spun on zir heel and headed into the kitchen in the back. "Darcie. Are you all set to get out of here?"

"Just about," Darcie called from her office. "Just have to lock up the safe."

Hari moved to lean against the doorframe, watching Darcie where she counted out the cash for the next day then stuffed everything, including the drawer, into the safe. Then she grabbed her phone and wallet, stuffed them into her pocket, and headed for the door with Hari trailing behind her.

"So, I know you don't want to talk about why you stopped baking," Hari said once they were loaded up on the subway and headed back toward zir apartment. "But would you be comfortable telling me why you started?"

Darcie took a breath, shifting enough that her jeans squeaked against the hard plastic seat, perhaps preparing herself to say that no, she was not comfortable discussing that, and call off the rest of their evening all together. Which would be horrible. Hari knew better than to make zir interactions feel like an interrogation, but ze had never really learned to stay zir curiosity.

Hari was just about to say forget it and go back to small talk to fill the void when Darcie let out a sigh. "My mother came from a long line of bakers in South Korea. When my grandparents immigrated to America, they brought that with them, and eomma took over from halabeoji. Then she handed the bakery down to me when she passed."

It was the most words Hari thought ze'd ever heard Darcie say consecutively. Hari sat with them a minute, because that seemed the respectful thing to do after such a story. Still, eventually, as they always did, the questions got the better of Hari.

"Did she tell you that you had to become a baker like her?"

"What?" Darcie stilled entirely, her hands clasped in her lap, her eyes going from where they'd been examining what must have been a truly interesting spot on the floor to Hari. "What do you mean?"

"I mean, before she passed, did your mom tell you that you had to become a baker? Did she never tell you that you could be anything else?"

"Well . . . no." Darcie's dark brows wrinkled at the center, her gaze flicking over Hari's face uncertainly. "She always told me I could choose whatever career path I wanted."

"Then, why did you become a baker?" Certain metaphorical cats had died for asking less questions than Hari was peppering Darcie with, ze knew that. But that didn't mean ze could make them stop coming.

Darcie looked back to that spot on the floor, the one that was in the middle distance and looked distinctly like a piece of gum that had been trod on by no less than fifty people. "It was . . . Hmm . . . " She pressed her lips together for a moment and then nodded as if confirming a memory. "It was fun . . . when I was younger. Baking made me happy."

Hari opened zir mouth, maybe to ask another inane question, one that might make Darcie clam up entirely. But then the speaker above their heads crackled, and the conductor announced their stop was coming up. At least, Hari was fairly certain that's what they'd said; it was often hard to tell in the older trains where the speaker system was so garbled it sounded more like a garbage disposal speaking than a person.

"I think that's us." Hari stood, grabbing the bar above their heads to brace for the stop.

"How can you be sure?"

Hari laughed, nose scrunching, and ze leaned in to bump zir shoulder lightly against Darcie's, making her grip tighten on the bar above them. "Cute."

Darcie ducked her head, finding her shoes suddenly very interesting, and Hari felt zir ears heat. Ze cleared zir throat and looked at where they were pulling up into the station.

"Right. Come on. YingYing and ZhanZhan will get cranky soon if they don't have any play time. Well . . . Ying-Ying will. ZhanZhan is probably napping." Hari shrugged, leading the way onto the platform and then up the escalator and out to street level. From there, it was a couple of blocks' walk before they reached Hari's building, and they spent it in an awkward silence that Hari quickly decided ze hated.

"So. Fair warning," Hari said, stopping in front of zir door, zir keys jangling nervously between zir fingers. "It's a bit of a mess. Today has been . . . It's been a bit of a hurricane, to be honest, and I didn't really have time to tidy up like I'd normally like. So like . . . a lot of my photography supplies are out. And YingYing decided it was an absolutely fantastic time to hide under the bed and just not come out, so I didn't really have time to clean up all their toys."

Why was ze talking so much?! Didn't Yuuki always say that if ze didn't draw attention to zir mess by telling people about it, people probably wouldn't even notice? Why couldn't Hari just shut up and let Darcie come to her own conclusions?

Was ze . . . Was ze nervous? No. That didn't make sense. Hari didn't get nervous. That wasn't who ze was.

"Oh, and I tried to make cupcakes earlier. So the kitchen is also a disaster."

"Tried?"

"Uh . . . yeah. My cousin gave me a recipe, and it looked simple enough, but . . . " Ze shrugged. *Damn it, Hari, just put the key in the door and let her inside. Stop standing in the hall yammering on like a complete lunatic. Can't you just be quiet?* "And then Aura and Eero told me I couldn't buy grocery store cupcakes to serve you. So yeah . . . no cupcakes."

Clearly not.

Darcie blinked, her lips twitching a little at the corners, and then she was laughing softly. More a chuckle than anything else. But it was a nice chuckle, all things considered.

"It's not . . . It's not that funny." Hari huffed.

Darcie shook her head, letting out another soft sound of laughter, before she took a breath in through her nose and then looked back to Hari with her eyes squeezed shut in a smile. A small smile. But a lovely one just the same. "How about I help you make the cupcakes?"

Hari felt zir jaw fall a little slack, completely of its own volition, zir breath stilling a little in zir throat, and zir brain blue screened.

Darcie tilted her head in question. And Hari cleared zir throat again. "Uh . . . yeah. That sounds . . . That sounds nice. Come on in."

Ze turned back to the door and ignored the way it

seemed suddenly impossible to get the key in the lock and the doorjamb that always seemed to stick at exactly the wrong time unstuck. Hari choked on a nervous laugh and forced the door with zir shoulder before standing back to gesture inside like some kind of outdated gentleman.

ELEVEN

With Hari, Darcie had learned to expect the unexpected. Nothing about Hari had been what she'd thought. Where ze had seemed brash, loud, and over-confident on the surface, Darcie had found Hari to be the opposite, at least in part. Ze could be brash, and loud, and a little cocky, but by and large, ze was a kind, considerate person. It was . . . jarring to say the least.

Hari's space was no less jarring. Where Darcie would have assumed that Hari would go all in aesthetic-wise, zir space seemed more a haphazard collection of things. A comfortable looking, overstuffed couch covered in arguably too many throw pillows. A dark wooden coffee table that looked as if it may have been handmade. Bookshelves lined the walls, stuffed with books and colorful knickknacks. And even an end table that looked like it might give out under the weight of tomes stacked atop it. It was sheer chaos. It was . . . exactly like Hari, Darcie realized.

"Like I said, sorry about the mess. I usually at least try to get all the rabbit toys up before I have company." Hari laughed nervously, nudging what appeared to be a wooden carrot toward a basket in the corner which must contain all the other rabbit toys.

"It's all right. I don't mind."

"Right then." Hari nodded, kicking off zir shoes on the mat by the door. "Bunnies first, or takeout first?"

"What?"

Hari nodded to a corner of the open living space, and there Darcie finally saw a large green china cabinet on one wall. Inside of it, with its nose pressed against the mesh and giving Darcie a look of utter indifference, was a big white rabbit. There was some thumping, and then a black rabbit shoved the white one out of the way to get a better look at their visitor.

"YingYing, be nice." Hari huffed, moving over to the hutch to shake a finger at the rabbits. "So, what do you say?"

"We should make the cupcakes first," Darcie's mouth said without her permission. Because the truth was, she didn't think she wanted to do anything outside of cuddling the ever-loving fluff out of that white rabbit.

"That's some good out-of-the-box thinking there, Darcie."

"They'll have to cool before we can put frosting on them," Darcie said, refusing to play into Hari's teasing. "We can make them, then order food, then play with the rabbits while we wait for them to cool and the food to get here."

Hari tilted zir head, a little smile on zir face. "Pragmatic. I like it! All right then, cupcakes first. But I need to let these little heathens out, or YingYing will throw a tantrum."

"What does a bunny tantrum look like?"

"Trust me, you don't want to find out." Hari laughed, crouching to unlatch the door in the lowest cabinet. As soon as the door was an inch open, there were several more thumps, then a black blur raced out of the opening to skid across the hardwood floor.

"Should I try to corral him?"

"No. Just let him go. He'll run himself out in a few minutes." Hari reached into the hutch to nudge the white rabbit out too. "Come on, ZhanZhan, come out and play."

Zhanzhan's ear twitched. Darcie didn't know much about rabbits, but she felt like the fluffy little critter was giving Hari an unimpressed stare.

"He's shy," Hari said by way of explanation. "Aren't you?" Hari scooped ZhanZhan up into zir arms, pressing zir face between his ears, and gave him a quick squeeze.

The rabbit's ear twitched again, his eyes meeting Darcie's in an expression of *I am merely tolerating this because ze feeds me.* Darcie choked back a laugh.

"Right then. Go keep YingYing out of trouble for me, will you?" Hari set the rabbit on the floor and gave it a nudge with zir socked foot. "Go on. You know if you don't, he'll only make trouble."

ZhanZhan gave another annoyed ear twitch, but then he departed, likely to keep his chaotic brother out of trouble. Or maybe to just sit and watch as YingYing got into it. Darcie wasn't entirely sure.

Either way, Hari stood from zir crouch, brushed imaginary lint off zir floor-length midnight blue skirt, and smiled. "Cupcakes?"

"Cupcakes." Darcie nodded. Hari led the way to a large white and glass kitchen with white marble countertops and glass cabinet fronts that did nothing to hide the clutter of mismatched dishware inside.

"I threw the fail-cakes away, so you don't have to look at them. But I think I have enough to make another batch of dough."

"Batter."

"What?"

"Cakes are made with batter. Cookies are made with dough."

"Oh. Right." Hari grinned, pulling out a big mixing bowl. "Sorry."

"Why are you apologizing?" Darcie moved to the fridge to pull out the required amount of eggs and milk. She turned to watch Hari shift from foot to foot, rubbing at the undercut at the base of her neck.

"For not knowing the difference?"

Darcie frowned a little. "That is not something to apologize for. You're learning, you're allowed to not know things."

"Oh." Hari blinked for a moment and then smiled brightly. "Okay then. I'll grab the cupcake pan."

Darcie nodded, finishing gathering ingredients. Once everything was on the spacious island, Darcie set to work measuring everything out. The recipe Yuuki had provided was fairly straightforward, no complicated fillings or additions. Just a traditional cupcake batter with lemon flavoring. "We'll mix the dry ingredients together first."

"Is that . . . what you're supposed to do?"

Darcie stopped, setting down the cup she'd been using to measure out the flour with a frown. "Did you not do that the first time?"

"I . . . " Hari stopped, letting out a chuckle as ze shifted. "I may have missed that part on the directions."

Darcie forced herself to let go of the measuring cup and not clutch the counter in annoyance. It wasn't Hari's fault ze didn't know better. Ze was learning now; Darcie would just have to be patient. "Did you put everything in the bowl together at once and try to mix it?"

"Yes?"

"I see. Well, for future reference, dry ingredients should be mixed together first, and then you add the wet ingredients one by one as per instructions. This allows the dry ingredients to be thoroughly combined so that you don't wind up with clumps of them in certain parts of your batter."

"Okay, that makes a lot of sense, actually." Hari moved onto zir toes to peer over Darcie's shoulder as she worked. "What's the salt for?"

"Everything has a little salt in it. It brings out the flavors."

"Huh. Interesting."

"Baking powder." Hari scooted the little container closer so that Darcie could scoop out the required amount and put it in with everything else. "Why did you choose lemon?"

Hari shrugged. "I thought it'd be refreshing since we're having pizza for dinner. Plus, when Yuuki does them, he makes a lemon meringue icing, and the blowtorch looks really cool."

Darcie blinked for a moment, a frown tugging at the corner of her lips. "Have you ever made a meringue before?"

"Well . . . no."

"We'll do a buttercream."

"But the blowtorch . . . "

"Meringues are too hard if you don't have a stand mixer. Next time, I'll bring my stand mixer, and we can try a meringue."

"Really?" Hari bounced on the balls of zir feet.

"Yes. Now, zest a lemon for me." Darcie picked up the lemon, tossing it a little one handed before passing it over to Hari.

"Aye aye!" Hari gave a little salute.

They worked in a companionable silence from then on.

Darcie asked for things and gave quiet instructions, and Hari followed along without so much as batting an eye. When the cupcakes were finally in the oven, they both leaned back against the counters.

"How long before we get to eat them?" Hari crouched down in front of the oven, peering in through the glass.

"We still have to put frosting on them." Darcie didn't have to see the pout that Hari shot her to know that zir lower lip was poking out. "They will taste better with frosting on them. Naked cupcakes are just muffins."

Hari looked up from where ze was crouching, zir face blooming into a wide smile, and then ze laughed softly. "Naked cupcakes. That's cute."

Darcie ducked her head, hiding her heated cheeks in her hair. "Come on. Let's make the frosting, then we can clean up."

Hari groaned but rose and moved to the island without further complaint. The frosting was finished in a matter of minutes, and Hari pulled out zir phone to call in their dinner order.

"Vegetarian, right?"

Darcie looked up from where she'd been putting the bowl of frosting in the fridge to look at Hari with widened eyes.

"You always ask for your food without meat. I just kind of assumed. So that's good, right?"

Darcie nodded and watched as Hari spoke to the person at the pizza place, ordering one medium veggie lover's, a set of breadsticks, and a small salad. When it was all done, ze put zir phone in zir pocket and clapped. "Let's go see what trouble ZhanZhan and YingYing have gotten into, yeah?"

Hari didn't wait for a response. Ze led Darcie back into the main living area, where ZhanZhan was sitting on the lower shelf of the coffee table, glaring underneath the couch. He looked irritated.

"Bet I know where YingYing got off to. Huh, Zhan-Zhan?" Hari flopped onto zir belly beside the coffee table to peer beneath the couch. "Make yourself comfortable on the floor, Darcie. ZhanZhan will be happy to have a lap that's not going to get up and run off at any second."

ZhanZhan's ear twitched, but he turned to watch Darcie sit in the middle of the floor with her back to one of the bookshelves. After a few moments of listening to Hari click zir tongue at the rabbit under the sofa to coax YingYing out, Zhan-Zhan seemed to grow bored and hopped down off the coffee table. He bounced over to Darcie, eyeing her suspiciously, gave her leg a sniff, and then promptly climbed into her lap.

ZhanZhan must have been a magic rabbit, Darcie would swear to it, for the moment he was in her lap and her fingers were knuckle-deep in soft fur, she found words she hadn't known were lying dormant in her throat. "An influencer."

"What?" Hari asked, lifting zir head and nearly bumping it on the coffee table.

"Why did you become an influencer? You asked me why I became a baker, why did you become an influencer?"

Hari shrugged, sitting up to lean against the couch, zir long legs splayed out in front of zir. "No real reason. I mean, it's not what I always wanted to be when I grew up or anything. I just sort of fell into it."

"What did you want to be when you grew up?" Darcie stroked ZhanZhan's long ears. They were surprisingly silky. Like a good minky blanket.

"Lots of things." Hari laughed a little. "An actress for a little while. A painter. A photographer. Oh, and for about a year after *Legally Blonde* came out, I wanted to be a lawyer. Elle Woods was . . . Well if you've seen *Legally Blonde*, then you'd know. She was my gay awakening, actually. After that, I knew I liked girls."

Darcie swallowed down the feeling of a frown threatening to overtake her lips. From what she'd seen of gifs and pictures, she was no Elle Woods. And she wasn't exactly sure why that mattered. "Because she was pretty?"

"What?" Hari frowned, then barked a laugh. "No. Because she was fierce. I've never really been attracted to people because of their looks. It's always been about who, not what, they are."

Darcie ducked her head to watch ZhanZhan's slow blink, because there was something too open and honest in Hari's expression then. Something she decided it would be best if she not look directly at, and maybe not discuss at all. Something too much like hope.

"I have not," she said instead of all the other things that she thought she might want to say. Like, *am I fierce?*

"Not what?"

"Seen *Legally Blonde*."

"What? Seriously?!"

Darcie nodded.

"Okay, so that's what we're watching once the food gets here. Screw sitting at the table like adults, we're going to curl up on the couch like heathens, eat pizza, and watch Elle put some old white guys in their place. Good?"

"Good." Darcie looked up, a soft smile twitching at her lips.

"Good. Now . . . I need to feed these little monsters before they start trying to chomp off our fingers."

Darcie's eyes widened, her hand jerking away from the

rabbit in her lap. ZhanZhan lifted his head to cut her an aggravated look.

Hari let out a loud laugh, shaking zir head. "You should have seen your face!"

Darcie glared.

"You know, you look exactly like ZhanZhan when you do that." Hari winked, rising to zir feet, zir skirt sweeping the floor as ze headed for the hutch to pour the rabbits some food. "It's cute."

TWELVE

I t was hard to tell how Darcie felt about things. Hari had made a study over the last few weeks of the subtle shifts in expression and tone, but even with all of that practice, it was still difficult to tell if Darcie liked the movie or not. Especially as she was apparently the type to just sit and watch a movie in utter silence. A feat Hari found oddly refreshing after years of having to watch movies with the subtitles on so ze could read what people were saying while Katsuko complained loudly about poor line delivery and shoddy writing. She also didn't check her phone or go online to figure out where she knew an actor from like Hari might have.

In fact, Darcie hadn't picked up her phone at all since showing up to Hari's apartment. Hari didn't even know there were people their age that could go an entire evening without checking their phone at least once. It was intense.

"So?" Hari asked when the final credits finally ran, shifting in zir seat on the couch. Ze had been sitting still too long. If Hari didn't get up and move soon, ze was likely to burst out of zir skin.

"Elle was fierce," Darcie confirmed, leaning forward to carefully stack her empty paper plate beneath Hari's. "I can see why you were attracted to her in your formative years."

"Right?" Hari grinned over at her, ignoring the awkward wording in favor of grabbing another breadstick to put on zir plate. "I'd say we should watch the second one, but it's arguably not as good. Which is a crying shame. Still, I've heard they're going to make a third one, so maybe they'll pull an *Aladdin*, where the second one is a dumpster fire but the third one is somehow even better than the first."

"Am I fierce?" Darcie blurted as if she'd been holding the words on her tongue for the last two hours. She didn't look at Hari, but Hari could see her hands twitching in her lap and the lobes of her ears turning red.

"I'd say so." Hari let a soft grin press a dimple into zir cheek and wrinkle zir eyes. Ze wasn't sure why Darcie was asking, but Hari could hope that maybe it was because she wanted Hari to like her. Maybe it was because Darcie liked Hari. Maybe it was . . . *No. Don't get ahead of yourself, Hari. Be cool.*

"Really?"

"What, really?!" Hari choked out the words. *Not cool. C'mon, Hari!* "What do you mean 'really'? You run a successful bakery. In the middle of Manhattan. By yourself. And have for years! You'd have to be fierce to do something like that."

"It was a family—"

"Nope. Don't want to hear it. I've seen many a family business go under in under an hour once they're passed down to another family member. Especially food places. The fact that you've kept Gyeong's going for . . . How many years?"

"Nine." Darcie ducked her head to hide behind her shoulder-length hair.

"Nine?! You've kept it open for almost a *decade* by *yourself?!*"

"Well, not by myself. After eomma passed, I had some help."

"Still! That's . . . I don't think I can count on one hand how many places in the city I know of that have lasted that long. Especially in the last few years, with how trendy food has gotten. It seems like every other day there's some new experimental cronut or fusion threatening to put everyone out of business if they don't jump on the bandwagon. Darcie . . . you must be one hell of a businesswoman." Was ze blushing? Oh god, ze was blushing. Hari cleared zir throat, hoping that Darcie wouldn't look up and notice. It wouldn't do for her to see the admiration shining in Hari's eyes. It wouldn't do for her to realize how absolutely gone on her Hari was already. If zir friends could only see zir making a complete and utter fool of zirself.

"The cupcakes should be cool enough now," Darcie said, her eyes fixed on some point on the coffee table. Probably the single ring from when Hari had first gotten the damn thing and not realized that condensation would leave its mark on wood. Ze used coasters now.

"What?" Hari shook zir head, looking away from the ring.

"We should be able to frost the cupcakes." Darcie stood from her seat and made her way back into the kitchen without another word.

"Uh. Right." Hari scrambled to follow behind her, leaving the half-eaten breadstick behind. "Do you think we could put some food coloring in the icing?"

"Why?" Darcie asked, her back to Hari where she was

carefully pressing a finger to the top of a cupcake in the fridge. Whatever temperature they were must have been cool enough because she pulled the tray out to set it on the counter.

"So we can make them pretty. We could like . . . pipe flowers and stuff onto them. I know you know how to do that. You could teach me."

Darcie looked down at the plain cupcakes, then up at Hari, and nodded. "What colors?"

"Oh! Purple, and red, and maybe some blue?"

"They are lemon." Darcie began to pull the cupcakes carefully from the tray.

"So?" Hari cocked zir head, tapping at the tip of zir nose, and then ze smiled. "Oh. What about sunflowers? Do you know how to pipe sunflowers?"

"I do."

"Would sunflowers go good on lemon cupcakes?"

Darcie looked down at the cupcakes, her fingers tapping on the marble counter. She nodded. "We will need yellow and brown icing. Where are your food colorings?"

"No green?"

"Let's keep it simple this time." She pulled the bowl of icing from the fridge as well. "I hope you have piping bag tips."

"Oh yeah, I bought a whole set!" Hari moved to grab everything from the drawer ze had stuffed it in after trying to make the kitchen look somewhat more tidy. "These will work, right?"

Darcie nodded. She grabbed a butter knife from the silverware drawer and started mixing the yellow icing. Once she had it a color she was happy with, she held the knife out to Hari. "I need you to spread a border around the edge of the top of the cupcake with yellow."

"A border?"

"Yes. With an empty space in the middle." She gave no further instruction, or reasoning, just grabbed another butter knife and took the bowl of icing she'd portioned off to begin creating brown.

Hari was halfway through the batch of cupcakes when she'd finished and set to work helping with the rest. When that was done, Darcie prepared a piping back with yellow icing.

"Watch me," she said and then carefully set to work creating a neat row of petals along one side of the cupcake. "You try."

Hari's brows pressed together, taking the bag and cupcake from her and trying with unsteady hands to replicate what she'd done. It was a disaster. A complete and utter disaster. "Well. That doesn't look like what you did at all."

Hari looked up from the monstrosity of icing ze had created to find Darcie pressing a hand to her lips.

"Are you . . . laughing at me?"

Darcie shook her head.

"Don't lie. You're laughing at me!" Hari laughed too. Darcie dropped her hand and let the soft sound of her laughter fill the kitchen. It was nice. Much nicer than any laugh Hari thought ze had ever heard before. Maybe because it was so rare. It spread like warmth from Hari's ears all the way down to zir toes.

"Here. Let me show you again." Darcie took the piping bag and another cupcake. Hari pressed in close, zir chin almost resting on Darcie's shoulder as ze watched. She made it look so easy.

"Wait. Wait. Go slower. You're going too fast." Hari chuckled.

Darcie turned her head to grin at zir over her shoulder

and repeated the process on five more petals in slow, methodical movements. "You try."

Another disaster.

And on and on it went.

They ran out of icing long before they ran out of cupcakes.

"They look like muppets." Hari leaned against the counter, licking icing off zir finger with a laugh.

"They do," Darcie choked around a giggle that sounded more gleeful than Hari thought ze had ever heard from her.

"What do we do with all the naked ones?" Hari surveyed the mess they had made of zir counter. If ze wasn't careful the icing might stain the marble, but ze would worry about that later. Right now, ze was simply enjoying the joy that was radiating off of Darcie. It was so painfully earnest, and Hari wanted to bask in it for as long as possible.

"Eomma always said that if you eat the mistakes, no one has to know about them."

"You know what? That's the kind of logical thinking I want from my bakers." Hari reached over, grabbing one of the more monstrous cupcakes, and stuffed half of it into zir mouth. Icing smeared across zir cheeks, and when ze looked up, Darcie was blinking wide-eyed at zir again. "What?"

Darcie reached over to grab one for herself and then did the same. A smile crinkled her eyes as she chewed.

"These are, like . . . really good." Hari savored the tart lemon zest mixing with the buttercream before swallowing and stuffing the other half of the cupcake into zir mouth. "They taste like sunshine."

"They do." Darcie wiped her mouth with a paper towel and took another bite, this one smaller, but she looked no less pleased with herself.

"It's because we had fun making them."

"What?" Darcie stopped, the remains of her over-iced cupcake still in her hand. "Why would that make a difference?"

"It just always seems to." Hari shrugged. "Did you stop baking because it wasn't fun anymore?"

Darcie set her cupcake down, a frown on her lips. "I should head home. I have to be in early to open up the bakery."

"Wait. What did I say? Darcie. Wait. I didn't mean anything by that."

She stopped at the door, her hand clutching the wall as she slipped her feet back into her shoes. "That's what this is about, isn't it?"

"What?" Hari still probably had icing on zir face. Ze looked ridiculous. But . . . ze had to stop Darcie from leaving. Not like this. Not when ze didn't even know what ze had done.

"Gwydion and their curse," Darcie bit out, her tone accusing. She wouldn't meet Hari's eyes. She wouldn't even look up from where she was putting on her shoes. And then she did look up, and that was worse. It was so much worse. It was a slap to the face. "That's why you invited me here. That's why you've been so nice to me. You just wanted to get close to me to . . . To what?" Darcie's chest was rising and falling in hard pants, her eyes glassy where they were directed just over Hari's shoulder, refusing to meet zir gaze.

"That's not what this is about. That's not—I didn't—" But ze couldn't really deny it, could ze? Ze couldn't say ze didn't know what Darcie was talking about, because ze did. And it must have shown all over zir face. Ze had never been good at hiding things like that.

"No. You know what? Fine. Pat yourself on the back for befriending the lonely, cursed girl. Run back to the witch and tell them that they're right, I am unhappy and it does affect everything I do. But don't—don't contact me again."

Hari blinked, zir hands falling to zir sides. "What?"

"I'll make your cousin's cake. But you have to make me a promise."

"What kind of promise?" Hari squeezed the words from zir too-tight throat. Like forcing something soft and vulnerable though a sharpened tube. It felt . . . This wasn't right. Ze hadn't *done* anything. Ze hadn't even said Gwydion's name, but Darcie had jumped to a conclusion . . . a not *entirely* incorrect conclusion.

"Don't show up at the bakery anymore. Don't call. Don't text. Let's keep this strictly professional." With her shoes finally on, Darcie grabbed the door. "That's all you ever really wanted anyway, right? For me to make that cake."

"No. That's not . . . That wasn't why."

"Oh, so it *was* because of the witch?" She stood in the doorframe, her eyes red from swallowing back tears.

"No! It was because . . . It was because . . . " The words got lost somewhere between Hari's brain and zir mouth. All ze needed to say was, 'It was because I liked you,' and ze couldn't even manage that much.

Darcie didn't give Hari time to get zir mouth to work properly. She spun, slammed the door, and Hari heard her stomping down the hallway on her way to the elevator.

Hari sank to the floor, pressing zir face into zir hands.

"ZhanZhan . . . YingYing . . . I think I messed up," ze whispered. "I think I messed up real bad."

THIRTEEN

"Why is it always one step forward and two steps back with you people?"

"Excuse me?" Darcie lifted her head to glare at Gwydion, who had appeared in the singular chair in front of Darcie's desk. They had one leg crossed over the other, and they were wearing a flowing sundress in a truly jarring shade of pink. "'You people'?"

"Humans. Well . . . fae do it too. Anyone mortal, really." Gwydion gave a one-shouldered shrug.

Darcie narrowed her eyes, debating if she really wanted to ask. On one side, knowing more about the person who cursed her might help her to undo the curse on her own. On the other, she really didn't care to know more about Gwydion. "Why are you here, Gwydion?"

"To try the bunny buns of course. But I asked the girl out front. Heather is really sweet, you should give that girl a raise by the by. And she said you hadn't made any in two weeks."

"No. I haven't." Darcie gripped her hands beneath the

desk hard enough that she felt her short nails digging into the meat of her palms.

"May I ask why?" Gwydion's head cocked like a very curious bird's, and they raised one red brow, but there was something in their gold gaze that seemed to say that they knew. They knew what had happened between Darcie and Hari, and they were here to scold her about it.

"That's not why you're here."

Gwydion raised the other brow, putting on a show of looking innocent. "What? Of course it is. I just want to know where the bunny buns are."

"I'm the only one who knows how to make them, and I'm not baking anymore." And there had been complaints, lots of complaints, about that fact.

"And this is why I said one step forward and two steps back. Honestly, mortals. What will I do with you?"

"Curse us, I suppose." Darcie turned back to her computer, determined to get her work done and ignore Gwydion. Maybe if she did it long enough, they would take the hint and leave.

Gwydion sighed, leaning back in their chair, and stretching their legs out for a moment before standing. "You should call Hari. I didn't have my hand in zir interest in you at all, and if you think I did . . . Well, you're not very bright."

Darcie clicked over to a word document pointedly and began typing, her fingers smacking against the keys as loudly as possible, even though she wasn't really writing anything. Just a string of incoherent nonsense.

Gwydion snorted. "Petty. Fine. Don't take my word for it. But you should at least let Hari apologize. People make mistakes. You can't just cut them out of your life entirely."

Darcie continued clacking at the keyboard until she was sure that Gwydion was gone. She leaned back in her chair, letting out a breath. She knew Hari was sorry. She knew Hari claimed to have nothing to do with Gwydion. Hari had been texting her every day for the last two weeks. But she was still mad. Or more accurately, she was still hurting. And she couldn't face Hari so long as that feeling sat in her chest like a weight.

Instead of acknowledging that feeling and trying to get to the root of it, she went back to work. There was always something to do at the bakery, and her apartment had received a deep clean at least twice in the weeks since she'd fought with Hari. It was better, she'd learned after eomma had gotten sick, to keep herself distracted. To focus on the things she could control and not let the ones she couldn't overwhelm her.

So, she'd silenced all notifications from Hari and was thankful when ze at least didn't come by the bakery. It would probably cause a scene, and Darcie didn't particularly want that. This was her place of business after all.

"Darcie," the other Sarah said, popping her head through the gap between the door and the doorframe.

"Yes?"

"There's someone here to see you. She says she's an old friend. She umm . . . I think it's someone you might have gone to culinary school with?" The other Sarah's eyebrows pressed together, causing a wrinkle between them.

"I'll be out in a minute." Darcie waited until she heard the other Sarah's retreating footsteps to have a mild panic attack. She pulled out her phone to check how she looked. Took down her hair. Put her hair back up. Pulled out a few loose strands to frame her face. Took down her hair again. Ruffled it with her fingers. Took a deep breath and tied it back in the short ponytail at the crown of her head.

The first thing she heard as she pressed the doors open

from the kitchen into the front of the bakery was, "Oh, it looks just the same as I remember it! You haven't changed a thing, have you Darcie?"

Darcie winced at the judgement that lined Lily's tone. It was hidden, deep under a faux layer of excitement and wonder, but Darcie had been Lily's best friend for most of their lives. She knew when Lily was hiding behind a smile.

"How quaint." Lily's dark eyes met Darcie's, the corners of her smile twitching into something that wasn't quite as nice as Lily wanted everyone to believe. A sneer.

"Lily." Darcie moved to the register, careful to keep the counter between herself and her "old friend". Hoping to avoid any physical contact. No such luck.

"And look at you, you haven't changed a bit either," Lily said, leaning over the counter to pull Darcie into a hug that was altogether too loose and ended in a condescending pat on the shoulder. The kind of hug Lily gave to people she truly disliked. "It's so good to see you."

Darcie pulled from the hug, pressing her palms into the counter to keep herself grounded. It did little good in the face of Lily, but it was something. It also was not enough to keep Darcie's mouth from saying things that her brain decided would be rude. "Why are you here, Lily?"

Lily gasped, clutching at her chest. "Darcie! You wound me! Can't I just come and seen an old friend? Honestly, do I need a reason?"

Yes, she did. She needed a reason, Darcie knew that. Lily had never done anything without a reason. It wasn't who she was. And usually that reason was to benefit herself. It had seemed harmless when they were eight years old and what Lily wanted was toys and attention. But when they were teenagers and what she had wanted was Darcie's girlfriend? Or when it was the award for best cake in culinary school? Well . . . Lily could be cutthroat. Darcie knew that better than anyone. She didn't say as much. She just stood, staring at a point over Lily's shoulder and hoping Lily would get to the actual reason she was in Gyeong's and leave as soon as possible.

Lily let out a sigh, her hand falling away from her chest where she tucked it into the pocket on her apron. "I just wanted to say hi. We're neighbors after all, aren't we?"

"So I've been told."

"And you didn't bother to come and visit me? I mean, I'm just right down the block, Darcie. You don't even have to leave K-town."

"And I'm exactly where you left me." Darcie forced herself not to clench her teeth together. Lily would notice. She always had. "You could have stopped in at any time."

"Yes, yes. I suppose I could have. But I was so very busy opening up Stargazer's, you know. And we've had a line out the door every day for months. I've hardly had time to sit down. Whereas Gyeong's is . . . Well."

Ah. That's what it was. She was there to rub the decline of Gyeong's in Darcie's face. Likely to try to intimidate her. To push her from the neighborhood so that she could remain the only Korean bakery in K-town. Darcie felt her jaw twitch with the need to grind her teeth. "If you're so busy, why are you here now?"

"Oh, we sold out for the day. So I figured I'd stop in and say hello. Like a good friend."

"Right." Yup. There it was. The bragging. Next would be the questions. The faux concern. The pity.

"But how are you? How is Gyeong's?"

Right on time. "We're doing fine."

"It's been months since I've seen a line here. Gosh . . . not since Stagazer's opened, I think. I hope I'm not . . . you know . . . " She leaned over the counter, cupping a hand around her mouth as if to tell Darcie a secret, and whispered, "Driving you out of business."

"We are doing fine." Darcie forced her face to go placid. To show Lily none of the emotion that was threatening to take over. But she knew Lily would see it. She would know how Darcie's heart had begun to feel heavy in her chest, how her joints had begun to ache with the strain of staying still when all she wanted to do was run. Run. Run.

"Ah, well, that's good. I'd hate for a quaint little place like this to go under. Especially when it's been here so long. Anyway, like I said, just came in to say hello. I'll be heading out now. Lots to do, you know? A successful bakery won't run itself, will it?"

"No. It will not."

The bell over the door chimed, and Darcie didn't even have time to see who it was before Hari announced zirself with, "I know. I know. You said don't stop by. But you aren't answering my texts, and I have this blogger I—" Hari stopped, pressing zir lips together. Ze looked worse for wear, with circles under zir eyes and zir maroon hair piled messily atop zir head. "Am I interrupting something?"

Lily's eyes drifted from Hari to Darcie. "Oh. I see," she said softly, a little smile tugging at the corners of her lips. "No, nothing important. I was just seeing myself out."

"Okay." Hari shifted onto zir heels, zir hands tucked into the back pockets of zir loose fitting jeans.

"See you later, Darcie." Lily pushed back from the counter and made her way back to the door. She stopped right in front of Hari. Her head tilted, dark, curly hair falling artfully across her face. "You're Hari's Hair-Raising Finds, aren't you?"

"Uh . . . yeah?" Hari smiled, holding zir hand out to Lily.

"Lily. I own Stargazer's, the bakery down the block. I've seen some of your pictures for Gyeong's, they're gorgeous." Lily shook Hari's hand, then turned to dig through her purse for a minute before holding a business card out to Hari. "Maybe you could contact me and we could work on something for my place?"

"Yeah. Sure. Maybe." Hari shrugged, taking the card and tucking in into zir pocket. "I'll be in touch."

"Super." Lily turned to give Darcie another halfhearted wave. The chime of the bell above the door announced her departure.

"Sooooo . . . " Hari rocked back on the heels of zir tennis shoes again. "Like I was just saying, I have this blogger I wanted to put you in touch with. They do a blog about historical places in New York City, and I think they'd be perfect for Gyeong's. You could talk about how it's a third generation—"

"I thought I told you not to come."

"You did." Hari blinked. "But you won't answer my texts."

"Email me the information for the blogger, and I will be in touch with them directly. Thank you for your assistance. Goodbye." Darcie pointed to the door again.

"Okay. Okay." Hari held zir hands up in surrender and spun back around to leave the way ze had come.

It wasn't until later that night, after everything had closed up and Darcie's employees had gone home, that she finally let herself think about the state Gyeong's was in. Lily was right. She was putting Darcie out of business. Little by little. And Darcie wasn't helping matters

She'd have to . . . If things didn't change, she'd have to do something drastic soon. Like let some people go. Darcie choked on a sob at the thought, letting her head fall to the desk.

FOURTEEN

Hari wasn't sure how many different ways ze could apologize. Nor how ze could convince Darcie that she'd been mistaken.

"You didn't do anything wrong," Eero said, sliding Hari's mug over to zir across the table. "You shouldn't have to apologize when you didn't do anything wrong."

"Then why do I feel like crap?" Hari wrapped zir fingers around the ceramic, letting the warmth seep into zir chilled hands. Ze had been so cold lately. Almost as cold as ze had been when ze'd lost zir first rabbit. Heartbreak was what Yuuki was calling it. He said that Hari had needed extra snuggles and blankets after zir father had left too, but Hari didn't remember that.

"Because you always take too much of other people's problems onto yourself, that's why." Eero sighed, running a hand through his short red hair. "Look, you tried to help her and it blew up in your face. It happens."

Hari opened zir mouth to argue.

"Yes, even to you." Eero waved away the protest. "You've just got to let it go. You can't keep carrying this around on you. Why don't you call that other baker? What was her name? Lila?"

"Lily."

"Right. Lily. Why don't you call Lily?"

"It's not about the fact that she's a baker, Eero." Hari grumbled into the lip of zir mug before taking a careful sip of the still too-hot coffee. "I just like her. She's funny."

"I know that. But I've seen Lindsey's place online, it's really cute. And everything she makes is perfect for pictures. Maybe you need a new project, and her bakery will distract you from Darcie. It can't hurt to try. Distractions are a great way to get over a breakup."

"Lily. It's not a breakup."

"Of course not."

"What if I don't want to get over it?"

Eero tsked, leaning over to ruffle Hari's hair. "Silly human, why wouldn't you?"

Hari swatted his hand away with another grumble, narrowing a glare on him. "This is why Blaze doesn't come to you when he and Fable are fighting."

"He and Fable don't fight. They *disagree*."

Hari leveled Eero with a flat look.

Eero sighed, letting his hands drop to the table between them. "Look, you have two choices. You can either sit here and sulk, letting all this"—he gestured to Hari's face and self —"awesome go to waste. Or you can throw yourself into a new project and see where it takes you. I personally suggest the latter, but that's between you and your camera phone."

"I'm not dating Lily."

"I didn't say you had to. Just go down to her bakery, take some pictures, see what you can do about spreading the word for her on social media. You know, let yourself enjoy your work instead of sitting here hovering over pictures of some truly heinous looking cupcakes. They're really ugly, Hari. I'm not even kidding." Eero stood from the table, stretching. "Just a thought."

"Where are you off to?"

"Aura and I are going down to the farmer's market. She said something about a candlemaker she really likes." Eero shrugged. "Do you need us to pick you up anything?"

"No. I'm all right." Hari sighed, flopping back in zir seat and drawing zir knees up onto the chair to press zir face into the fuzzy fabric of zir rabbit pajama pants. "I'm just going to take the day to wallow."

"You've been doing that a lot lately."

Hari glared sullenly through the gap between zir knees and hair.

Eero moved to ruffle zir hair again. "Get up. Take a shower. Call Louise."

"Now I just think you're doing it on purpose."

"Maybe I am. Maybe I'm not. No way to know." Eero winked.

"You're definitely doing it on purpose."

"Either way, if I come back by this apartment after we get done at the farmer's market and you're still here sulking, there will be trouble."

"Not sulking."

"I'll call Blaze and make him drag you out on a run with him."

"Don't do thaaaaaaat."

Eero gave Hari one final, vaguely threatening head tilt and left.

Hari huffed, and puffed, and grumbled, and groaned, but ze dragged zirself from zir chair and into the shower. Because ultimately, Eero was right. A new project would be the key to getting Hari out of zir funk. It wouldn't completely solve the sinking feeling somewhere along where ze thought zir spleen might be located, according to the internet, but it would be a good distraction until Hari could officially get over Darcie. Or until Darcie decided to listen to sense. Whichever came first.

With zir hair wrapped in a towel, which was slowly turning pink from zir hair dye, Hari pulled out the card Lily had given zir and made the call.

Two hours later, Hari found zirself sitting across a table in the packed little dining area of Stargazer's with a plate of Lily's "favorites" in front of zir. They were all objectively adorable, but Hari just couldn't find it within zirself to take a bite. Not yet. It felt like a betrayal. Which . . . was stupid. It was stupid. Hari had no contract with Darcie. They didn't have a relationship. They didn't have anything. But somehow, Hari couldn't get that expression Darcie had been wearing when Lily had handed Hari her card out of zir head. It was going to haunt Hari, and there was nothing ze could do about it.

"So, how do you know Darcie?" Lily asked, leaning forward to fix Hari with a sunny smile. It was a nice smile. The kind you'd find in the stock photos they used in picture frames. But Lily's eyes didn't crinkle with it. Just like the stock photos.

"I had read a review about Darcie's mochi buns and wanted to see what all the fuss was about. Then my cousin decided to have Darcie make his wedding cake." Hari looked down at the selection of pastries. They would photograph well. But they were almost too perfect. Almost too cute. Almost . . . fake.

"Ah. I see. But you've been taking pictures for her for a while now. I keep seeing it pop up on your feed. Did you sign a contract with her or . . . ?"

"Oh no. Nothing like that. We're just . . . or we *were* just friends." The words made something acidic eat away at the lining of Hari's stomach. Ze shouldn't have come. This was a bad idea. Such a bad idea. Why had ze let Eero talk zir into this?

Lily nodded, her face morphing into an expression of empathy and understanding. "Darcie can be difficult some-times. She's a good person, I just think . . . " Lily looked down at her hands where they rested, folded on the table, as she took a moment to gather her words. "I just think she gets in her own way a lot."

"Yeah . . . maybe that's it." Hari forced zirself to sit up straighter and pull on a smile ze didn't really feel. "But enough about that. What did you want to talk about? I assume it's about getting some shots of these loooovely pastries. Am I allowed to eat the props?"

Lily laughed, her hands unclenching as she leaned over the table to nudge the tray closer to Hari. "You certainly may eat the props."

"Now that's what I like to hear!" Hari grabbed one of the gyeran-ppang from the tray and set it on the little pastry bag it had come in before leaning back to take a quick picture with zir phone. Ze took a bite, then another picture before humming happily around the fluffy pancake and still-runny egg yolk. It was good. Very good. Almost as good as Darcie's, but it was still missing . . . something. A little of the heart and soul that went into every Gyeong pastry maybe? Or maybe it was just cinnamon? Hari wasn't sure. Ze posted about it right away and then turned zir phone on silent to get back to the meeting at hand. "So, what is it you had in mind?"

"A partnership, of sorts. We need pictures for the website, better than the ones I've been able to take. And then I was thinking maybe a month of promotion—not every day, as I'm sure your audience would get tired of it. But I'd love a feature on your blog, and maybe while you're here taking shots for the website, you could feature some of our more . . . photogenic pastries on your social channels? I'd pay, of course. I have a small budget set aside for promotional work." Lily's tone had gone all business.

"What's the exclusivity like?" Hari dusted zir hands off on a napkin.

"I wouldn't want you working with another bakery during the month. Just to keep it so people don't get confused." Lily flapped her hand through the air, brushing away such a thought. "I'm sure you understand."

"I do."

"I knew you would. So, what do you say?"

It wasn't like Darcie was currently talking to zir anyway. And besides, this was just business, Hari reasoned. "Sure. Why not?" Lily held out her hand, and Hari took it to give it a firm shake. "Do you need me to sign anything?"

"No. I don't think we need all that. You're a professional, I trust your integrity."

"I'll get the paperwork sent over this evening then. I have something I like my clients to fill out just so I know what they want from the shoots, and it protects me if someone decides not to pay their bill. Nothing serious." Hari picked up the gyeran-ppang and took another slow bite to savor it. It still wasn't right. There was still something off, but ze couldn't quite put zir finger on it. Ze would need more experimentation, and clearly ze was going to get it.

"Perfect! Until then, why don't I give you a little tour, huh? Maybe it'll spark some ideas?" Lily stood from her seat, plucking a red bean bun off the tray and taking a big bite as she led Hari back to the kitchen.

It was a productive meeting. The kind that Hari liked to have with zir clients. The kind that would lead to beautiful photographs and more business for the client. The kind that might lead to more clients if Hari played zir cards right.

Still, ze felt almost hollow heading back home with a sack full of Stargazer's baked goods hanging from zir fist. Hollowed out enough to make the kind of mistake that ze knew would come back to haunt zir as soon as ze picked up the phone. Because ze was an idiot. Because ze had never learned that rebounds were hell. Because ze hated being alone.

"You know, I was thinking," Lily said into zir ear. "There's no reason this has to be strictly professional. I mean, I didn't make you sign anything. So why don't we meet up for dinner and go over this paperwork? It'll be easier for me to explain the overall aesthetic in person. Plus, I'd like to pick your brain a little more. Get to know the Hari behind Hari's Hair-Raising Finds. What do you say?"

And Hari realized there really was no reason not to, was there? Ze wasn't dating Darcie. Ze wasn't dating *anyone*, hadn't been for at least a year at that point. And besides, hadn't Eero said that Hari should go out and try to distract zirself? Lily was certainly pretty enough to be a distraction. Add to all that Hari's inability to ever say 'no' to people and you had the perfect storm.

"Sure. Why not?"

FIFTEEN

I t shouldn't have been a surprise when the texts stopped coming. Darcie had known it would happen. She had pushed Hari away. She had cut Hari off. No one would keep trying after all that. Not when there were other better, more interesting people to talk to. But it did. And not only did it surprise her, it also surprised her how much it hurt. It was like an ache had settled into her chest, right alongside the one left behind by eomma.

"You can't keep doing this," a voice called from the office door. There were no windows in the little room, no indication of what time it was. Only a desk, a computer, and the pictures left over from when it had been eomma's. Darcie had never even bothered to try to personalize it for herself, which she knew was arguably not healthy, but she couldn't find it within herself to care. Not when there were other things to worry about.

"Keep doing what?" Darcie asked, shifting in her seat so she could see Heather from around the monitor.

"Hiding in here." Heather was young, young enough to not be properly afraid of her boss. Or maybe it was that, over the last couple of months, Darcie had found herself forming some kind of companionship with the girls in the shop. Hari had . . . Hari had helped with that. Ze had made it seem like a good idea to be friendlier with them.

"I'm not hiding." Darcie ducked back behind the monitor to avoid eye contact. Heather didn't say anything, but Darcie could still see her shadow on the floor in front of the door. Her shadow looked . . . unimpressed, if shadows could look anything. "What do you think I'm hiding from?"

Heather muttered something under her breath that sounded suspiciously like, "I swear, old people."

"What was that?"

"I have to go back to school when the semester starts back up. That's in a couple of weeks. You either need to hire another baker, or you need to do it yourself."

"Are you quitting?"

"No. But I won't be able to work during the week, you know that. I told you that when I started here at the beginning of the summer."

Darcie grunted, tapping her fingers hard enough on the keyboard in front of her to make herself sound busy. It didn't make the shadow of Heather go away.

When Darcie refused to further acknowledge her, she heard Heather sigh, and turn to head back into the kitchen, but not before saying, "You know, you were getting better there for a bit. Maybe you should just apologize to Hari."

Darcie leaned forward, pressing her forehead to the cold desk. It did absolutely nothing for her headache, but her head suddenly felt so very heavy. She didn't know how long she sat there trying to breathe through whatever emotion it was that was clogging up her insides, but when she lifted her head again, silence had fallen in the kitchen beyond her office. The girls had gone home and left her to her own devices. They hadn't invited her out to dinner. They hadn't even bothered to say goodbye. They had just . . . gone. Which was . . . fine. It was fine. They were her employees, not her friends. And like Heather had said, when the semester started back up, most of them would be too busy with classes to help with the bakery anyway.

"That'll be for the better," Darcie told herself, but it sounded like a lie even to her own ears.

"You won't have to bother paying them. You can recoup some of your costs." She rose from the desk, ignoring the silence and going to check on the dough that had been set to rise for the following day.

WEDNESDAYS WERE ALWAYS SLOW, Darcie reasoned. There was no reason to connect the emptiness of the shop with what was going on with Darcie. No reason to think that—

"Stale." The smack of a newspaper broke Darcie from her thoughts where not even the bell above the door had. She looked down at the page that had been folded over to a review of Gyeong's. "You're stale."

Darcie looked up from the paper to narrow her eyes on Lily. "Did you come here just to show me this? I can buy the paper if I want to read what some second-rate hipster food snob who spends all their time chasing the next cronut thinks of my bakery."

Lily looked positively giddy at this reaction, which just made Darcie's stomach roll. She'd played right into Lily's hands. "Of course."

"As much as I appreciate the free litterbox liner, what do you want, Lily?"

"You don't own a cat," Lily said, accusing, but her eyes were still bright with whatever she thought she was going to get from Darcie.

"You don't know that. I could have adopted a cat."

Lily snorted.

"You didn't answer my question. Why are you here?"

"I heard you're looking for a baker."

"And, what? You came to offer your services? Don't you have your own shop to run?"

Lily's expression had gone soft around the edges, complicated. Like she was actually experiencing an Emotion aside from her rabid competitiveness. Whatever it was, Darcie blinked and it was gone. "No. I came to make you an offer."

"Of course you did." Darcie leaned down to grab a roll of paper towels from under the counter. She went to wipe down the tables, as if they weren't still clean from last night. But she needed something to do with her hands, and she kind of hoped looking busy would get Lily out of there faster.

"Since you're not baking anymore, why not sell me your family recipe book?"

Darcie stopped, her hand gripping the back of the chair nearest the window—Hari's chair—hard enough that she felt the wood creak beneath her palm. "What?!"

"If you're not baking them, someone should be." Lily shrugged.

Darcie swallowed down a growl as it crawled up her throat. She couldn't throw the bottle of cleaner at Lily's face. That would be a lawsuit waiting to happen. But that didn't mean she didn't *want* to. How had she ever been friends with someone who would suggest *that*?

"Look," Lily said, much closer now, though Darcie

hadn't tracked her progress across the room. "I don't know what's up with you lately. But your mom's recipes, your family's recipes, they should be made by someone who will appreciate them. Not some rando baker looking to make an hourly wage. They should be made by someone who loves them. And if you're not going to do it, it seems a waste for you to—"

"Get out. Now," Darcie growled, her hands shaking around the bottle of cleaner and wadded up paper towel. "Get out and don't come back."

"What? I'm only trying to—"

"To what, Lily? Pretend that we're friends long enough that you can steal my legacy out from under my nose?"

"Well, if you aren't using it! Honestly, you're so stubborn sometimes! Why not take the money and do something else? Do something that makes you happy!"

"I said *get out*!"

"Fine. Let your legacy waste away, and let it take you with it. See if I care!"

And then Lily was gone, and Darcie collapsed into the chair, the bottle of cleaner and paper towels smacking against the floor beneath her as she pressed her face into the still damp table and let herself cry for . . . perhaps the first time in a long time. Such a long time.

The sun set, leaving only the warmth of streetlamps to light the sidewalks outside, and still Darcie sat there, sobbing into the table. She sat there until her face was crusty and dry from the salt, and her throat hurt from swallowing too hard around the emotion. And then she stood up, scrubbed at her face with her sleeves, locked up, and went back to the kitchen.

Stale. She'd show them *stale*.

IN THE MORNING, the glass case was full to bursting with pastries, and Darcie stood behind the register with deep bags under her eyes. But everything she'd made had at least tasted like it should. Maybe not as good as eomma had made it, but it was good enough. Enough to prove she could do it. Enough to remove the want ad for a baker.

"I'm glad to see you baking again," Gwydion said. The bell over the door hadn't tinkled, but suddenly they were there, bright hair tied back into a high ponytail, lips spread into a soft smile. "It looks good on you."

"Does that mean you're going to remove my curse?"

Gwydion laughed, the sound like wind chimes. "Oh, heavens no, child." They shook their head. "You're still not happy, are you?"

Darcie sniffed, nodding to the full display case. "Try one."

"I will, but honey, determination isn't happiness. This is competitiveness, plain and simple. And while I'm sure they taste fine, they won't ever be as good as they used to be until you're really truly happy making them. And if you can't be happy making them, maybe you should find something else to do."

"I like baking," Darcie said, arguing like a child with an adult who seemed to think they were right all the time. And in fact, maybe Gwydion was more of an adult than she was. They had been around . . . Well, Darcie wasn't sure how long, but she had her suspicions.

"Is liking it enough? Would your eomma have been happy knowing you would just like running a bakery, not love it like she had? This is . . . Hmm . . . " Gwydion thought, pressing their lips together. "Running a bakery is too big a commitment to only do because you like it and because you feel like you have to. You should be happy doing it. You should love it."

Darcie opened her mouth to argue again, and Gwydion shook their head.

"Just think about it, all right? Think about what about when baking made you happy, use that. And until then . . . I'd like half a dozen kkwabaegi. I'm meeting with my writer's circle today, and we're going to need the sugar." Gwydion winked.

Darcie rolled her eyes and went to retrieve the ordered pastries.

WHAT GWYDION HAD SAID HAD MADE TOO much sense. Which was why Darcie had obviously ignored it and thrown herself into her baking like never before. She measured everything down to the ounce and never once deviated from the recipes, hoping that in doing so, she could capture some of that magic that eomma had always filled her pastries with.

So much so that she totally forgot about the meeting with Hari, Yuuki, and Alrik to discuss the wedding cake the following week. Up until the moment when Hari showed up in a pair of huge cat eye sunglasses, an over-sized sweater hanging off one shoulder, and leggings. Ze yawned into zir wrist as ze took a seat at the table that Darcie had inexplicably been unable to move from the window.

"I'm sorry, are we keeping you up, sleeping beauty?" a young girl with long dark hair and Hari's nose asked as she sat across from zir.

"It was a late shoot last night," Hari mumbled into the lip of zir coffee cup.

"You could have just told her no. You didn't have to—"

Hari cut her a look over the top of her sunglasses, and the girl stopped as Darcie made her way over to them. "Darcie!" Hari grinned too brightly. Fake—it was so fake, it made Darcie's hair stand on end. "How good to see you again. We're just here for a decoration meeting. Yuuki and Alrik won't be joining us, they had to work, so they sent along some ideas. But this is my little sister, Katsuko."

"Little," Katsuko muttered under her breath before meeting Darcie's gaze with an assessing look. "You're the baker?"

Hari kicked Katsuko under the table. Katsuko kicked Hari back.

"Yeah. I'll go get some samples," Darcie said, excusing herself from whatever was going on between the siblings. It would probably be better if she didn't get involved. When she came back out with the book of pictures, the siblings were aggressively mouthing things at each other. Darcie cleared her throat. "Here's the book of cakes we've done in the past."

The binder smacked against the lacquered table, and Hari opened it to flip through the pages too quickly. Ze got to the end of the book in record time and shut the binder without even bothering to hand it over to zir sister. "Where are the cakes *you've* done?"

"What?"

"These are all from the nineties at the latest. Where are the pictures of cakes you've done? What does your decorating style look like?" Hari's tone had gone strangely . . . businesslike. Darcie didn't like it.

"I can do whatever you want me to do." Darcie swallowed around the feeling of a scream crawling up her throat. There seemed to be an awful lot of noises wanting to crawl up her throat, and she decided she didn't like that either.

"I trust you with the design. I'll send you pictures of the samples of decorations and flowers we have. I'm sure you can come up with something beautiful based on that."

"That's not really how I work." Darcie straightened her spine. "I usually just do one of the designs from the book."

"Well, that won't be good enough." Hari lowered zir sunglasses to meet Darcie's gaze with a hard look. "We don't want something generic. If we wanted something generic, we'd go to the grocery store."

"What?" Darcie choked.

"You heard me." Hari stood up. Zir voice had gone strangely cold, detached. Like . . . like ze didn't care. Darcie's joints froze with the frost in the words. "I'll have the samples sent over to you by the end of the week. I look forward to seeing what you come up with. If you can't come up with something suitable, I guess we'll just have to go with another baker."

Darcie was still choking on her own tongue by the time the door swung shut behind the siblings.

"What?!" she screamed at the closed door. So much for swallowing it down. Then she took a breath, closed her eyes, and forced herself to calm down. "All right, Darcie, you got this. Just . . . do like you used to when eomma would let you help design the cakes."

Yeah. She could do this. She could definitely do this.

SIXTEEN

"That," Katsuko said, nudging Hari with the toe of her slipper from where they lay side by side on the rug in Hari's studio, "was the most mentally painful thing I've ever had to witness. And I had to watch you go through puberty."

"Hey! Rude!" Hari smacked her with the prop pillow ze had been hugging to zir chest for the last . . . ze looked at zir watch to check the time. Hour. The last hour. Maybe ze had been sulking long enough. "But . . . I know."

"Why didn't you just tell her she hurt your feelings?"

"Because we aren't third graders. Adults don't just tell people that they're upset because they've been dumped." Hari really needed to get up. Ze needed to get up and do something to distract zirself from the fact that ze had probably just made the whole situation with Darcie more of a mess. Ze hadn't known that was possible, and yet, here they were.

"Honestly, for a minute there, I thought you two were just going to kiss and make up, and I could stop watching you sulk." Katsuko had a distinctly . . . honest way of putting things. Brutally so, if you asked Hari. Hari had thought ze would have gotten used to it after so many years of being her older sibling, but the sting never seemed to wear off. Although it was always funny when Katsuko turned that brutal honesty on an unsuspecting victim that was *not* Hari, so ze supposed there was that.

"I'm seeing someone. Sort of."

"Ugh, Lily. Don't remind me." Katsuko threw an arm over her face.

"Yes. Lily. What's wrong with Lily?" Hari sat up to look down at zir sister with zir brows raised.

"She smiles too much, it's gross."

"There's nothing wrong with smiling. That just means she's happy."

"I want to go on record as saying, I did not mean for you to start *dating* the new baker," Eero said from . . . somewhere. Hari wasn't sure where; ze and Katsuko had had a couple rounds of sake and called him before laying down in the middle of the thick rug in the studio, where Hari's phone had promptly been lost. And honestly, he'd been quiet so long Hari, had thought he'd either fallen asleep or hung up. Or at least Hari was hoping he had. No one needed to listen to the Atsushi siblings go down one of their "relationships suck" spirals.

"You told me to distract myself," Hari said, even though ze knew it was a weak excuse. Hari had known it was a bad idea before ze had even gone to the first dinner with Lily. Rebounds were never a good idea. They never solved anything. But still, Hari kept trying. Probably because ze hated being alone after a breakup.

"That doesn't mean date her!" Katsuko shouted, smacking Hari in the face with one of the minky blankets from the cabinet in the corner.

Hari threw the blanket across the room and glared at Katsuko, who just reached for another one. Hari lifted a finger to point at Katsuko, zir eyes narrowing. "Don't."

"Besides, all she wanted to do the other night was talk crap about your ex. Huge red flag, bro," Eero said from somewhere near the bin of fake flowers. How had Hari's phone gotten all the way over there? Had Katsuko thrown it?

"Darcie isn't my ex." She wasn't, Hari reminded zirself. They had had that one evening where they had hung out, as friends, made really delicious cupcakes, and talked about *Legally Blonde*. They hadn't even kissed. That wasn't a date.

"Yeah, but you want her to be." Katsuko giggled, a little too giddy for the fact that it had been at least an hour since their last drink. But then, it was getting rather late, and Hari could feel the punch-drunk feeling of 2 a.m. crawling behind zir eyes. So maybe it was that.

"I didn't want her to be my ex."

"No, you wanted her to be your giiiiiirlfriend," Eero sang. Hari desperately needed to find the phone so ze could hang up. It was bad enough to have zirself exposed and laid bare in front of zir sister. Ze didn't need Eero to see all the cracks and crevices that Hari kept carefully hidden too.

"Yeah, well, what about you and Aura? Have you asked her out yet?"

"Oh, would you look at the time? I have an early shift at the firehouse tomorrow. Night, Atsushi siblings! Love you!" And then Hari heard the soft click of the line going dead.

Silence followed. Hari wondered if Katsuko had fallen asleep, but ze didn't want to check for fear of waking her up. Because ze couldn't escape the conversation with Katsuko as ze had with Eero. Katsuko knew that trick too well. So maybe if she had fallen asleep, ze could just—

"You really like her, don't you?"

Ah, damn. "Does it matter at this point? I'm dating Lily."

"No. You've gone on dates with Lily." Katsuko turned her head so she could look at Hari through the deep shag of the carpet. Hari could only see one dark brown eye through the fibers, but that eye was staring at zir so intensely, it bellied the humor in the situation.

"I know." Hari turned to stare up at the ceiling. It was easier than meeting zir sister's eyes. Katsuko knew too much, saw too much—she always had.

"You don't have to keep going out with her if you don't want to." Katsuko said it like it was the most reasonable thing in the world. It wasn't, they both knew that.

"What about Blake?"

"What *about* Blake?" Katsuko countered, rolling back onto her back so she didn't have to look at Hari for this conversation. Hari knew the feeling all too well.

"What's going on with you guys?"

"Med school." Katsuko grabbed the blanket she'd been planning to throw at Hari and covered her face with it. "Are you sure that witch didn't curse us too? I mean, Yuuki fell in love with a cat, you and Darcie are . . . whatever you are, and I'm . . . " She waved her hand through the air, gesturing to herself.

"Amazing? Brilliant? The best damn comedian in Manhattan? Going places?"

"Being ignored in favor of books about gastrointestinal diseases." Katsuko wrinkled her nose.

"I notice you didn't argue with me about you being the

best." Hari smiled a little, perhaps the first real smile in weeks.

"Should I have?"

"I guess not."

The hush of New York City at 2 a.m. settled around them for a long moment. Just the distant sounds of traffic and a city that, while it never slept, at least slowed down. Hari loved this time of night, when everything settled into a slow crawl. When the world outside was hazy with tiredness and sleep, softened around the edges and waiting for the rise of a new day. Ze never felt a peace like ze did at 2 a.m. on a weekday in New York City.

"Hey, Hari," Katsuko called across the distance, her fingers reaching out to grab at Hari's and lace them together.

"Yeah?"

"I love you."

Hari let out a breath, squeezing zir sister's hand a little and closing zir eyes. They didn't say it a lot. Only in these quiet moments, where the world couldn't hear. But Hari always knew. Because sometimes you didn't need to say it. Sometimes your actions spoke louder than words ever could.

"I love you too, KitKat."

"I DON'T USUALLY DO this, but . . . " Lily trailed off, her fingers tapping on the steel table in the middle of the kitchen. There was a smile on her face, something shy and soft that made Hari almost think maybe Lily really liked zir. The thought felt strange. Hari hadn't been fooling zirself before; ze knew that ze and Lily were using each other. For Hari, it was about rebounding from Darcie, distracting zirself. And Lily had her own motivations. It was better that way, Hari had convinced zirself. "Well, I just thought it'd be fun. One last hoorah before our month is done."

"What?" Hari asked. Was Lily dumping zir? Why did that hurt? It shouldn't hurt.

"I thought we could make one of my recipes . . . together?" Lily was blushing, the color high on her cheeks.

Hari felt zir phone burning a hole in zir pocket. The phone that still had pictures of the truly horrible cupcakes ze had made with Darcie. The ones that ze had put in the freezer and been unable to throw away. Katsuko had threatened to do it for zir the other night. There had been a fight. That's why they'd wound up tipsy on the floor of Hari's studio.

"You don't have to if you don't want. I just thought it'd be . . . fun." Lily shrugged, her fingers tightening around a branded binder, the Stargazer's logo burned purple into the cover.

"No. I'd like that. I'd like that a lot." Hari forced the words past zir dry throat. Ze didn't know why it felt like Lily was trying to replace the memory of those horrible cupcakes, but Hari didn't have time to think about it. Not when . . . Not when Lily looked at zir like that. So vulnerable, and soft. Hari liked that look, wanted more of it, even if it was on the wrong person.

"Great. Then you tell me what you want to make, and I'll make a copy of the recipe for you."

"Right. Okay." Hari nodded, a little grin dimpling zir cheek. It was—It would be nice, ze decided. To have this with someone else, someone who maybe really liked zir. "Can I look through and pick?"

Lily nodded, sliding the binder across to Hari. The binder felt heavier than Hari had expected it to, like the weight of expectation lived in it. Running zir fingers over the cover, ze smiled across at Lily and then opened it. The first recipe was innocuous enough, standard fair for any bakery: a croissant. It was handwritten in elegant cursive. The next was something a little more specialized, typed on a typewriter and then photocopied. And on and on it went, each page a little different, each from a different time, a different person, Lily's family maybe. Or her travels. Hari couldn't—

Wait.

Hari knew that handwriting. Ze had seen it before. Not for more than a handful of minutes at a time. But ze knew it. It was etched into zir memory from a handwritten menu behind a glass case in desperate need of a coat of paint.

"Lily."

"Huh?" Lily asked, looking up from her phone.

"How did you get a Gyeong's recipe?" Were Hari's hands shaking? They felt like they were shaking. Ze let out a breath, trying to force them to stop, but it didn't help.

"That's not a Gyeong's recipe." Lily ducked back to her phone, refusing to meet Hari's gaze.

"It is. I recognize Darcie's grandfather's handwriting. This is a Gyeong recipe. Have you been . . . Have you been selling it?" Something disgusted and sick twisted in Hari's stomach.

"You can't prove it is." Lily reached over to take the binder, snapping it shut on Hari's fingers. Hari jerked them back, zir eyes narrowing on Lily. "Darcie's eomma gave it to me before she passed."

"Lily. It's wrong."

Lily shrugged.

"All the others, are they yours at all? Or did they come from other people's families?"

Another careless shrug.

"Does Darcie know you're using her family's recipes? How many do you have?" Hari reached for the binder again, intending to rip it from Lily's hands and find out for zirself.

Lily slid the binder from the table, pulling it to her chest to keep Hari from touching it further. Hari let zir hands fall limp against the cold metal table. It didn't matter. Lily was right, ze couldn't prove it. That thought made something sick twist in zir stomach.

"You're . . . You're putting her out of business with her own legacy!"

"She's putting herself out of business by not letting herself move with the times."

"We're done. I'm terminating our contract, and I'm deleting everything I've posted about Stargazer's. I'll have your money returned to you by the end of the week."

"Oh, come on, Hari, it's just business." Lily rolled her eyes.

"No. It's not. And I think you know that." Hari shook zir head, already gathering up zir messenger bag and stuffing zir camera inside. Ze moved to the door, not waiting for Lily to stop her. Although she still hadn't moved from where she was clutching the recipe book to her chest. "Honestly, Lily, I thought you were better than this."

"Are you going to try to expose me?" She honestly sounded a little nervous about it. Like if anyone could, it would be Hari.

"No. I'm not . . . I won't throw you under the bus like that." Hari's fingers gripped the swinging door of the kitchen harder than ze had ever held onto anything in zir life.

"Then what are you going to do?"

Hari felt like ze was swaying on zir feet. Ze wasn't even sure why. Ze had known Lily was . . . something. Not the best person? Maybe. "I'm not sure yet. Maybe I'll just . . . Maybe I'll just help Darcie push you out of the neighborhood."

Lily snorted. "Yeah, if she lets you."

"Anything's better than watching you shut her down with stolen recipes," Hari said through a clenched jaw.

"Good luck with that."

"I don't think I'll need it."

"Need what?"

"Luck." Hari shrugged, then ze turned and left. Ze would have to call Darcie. Ze would need to contact Katsuko. Ze would . . . First, ze needed to do some drastic clean-up of zir social channels.

SEVENTEEN

Cutting down the menu was the obvious choice, Darcie told herself. But even as she raised the pen to begin marking things off their daily list of items, she couldn't seem to force it to meet paper. She couldn't even remember the last time they'd sold some of these items. Maybe not since before eomma had passed. Maybe not since she'd made the menu back in the eighties, before Darcie was born, retracing halabeoji's handwriting. But that was the thing, wasn't it? Eomma had made this menu. It had been the one she'd worked up after she'd taken over for halabeoji. And Darcie couldn't bring herself to destroy what eomma had made, even in the name of saving everything else.

She dropped the pen, letting it roll dangerously close to the edge of her desk without its cap to stop it, and sat back in her chair. She couldn't do it. She'd have to think of something else. Maybe she could cut the hours they were open. Or remove some of the lightbulbs in the fixtures in the back to lower their energy consumption. Or . . . something. There had to be another way to cut costs without destroying the menu eomma had built, even if she knew that thought was silly.

Eomma would want her to do whatever she had to to save Gyeong's. She would want Darcie to tear it apart and remake it into something that would survive the next generation. To keep Gyeong's in New York for as long as possible. And in not doing that, in not putting pen to paper, Darcie had failed her.

Darcie grabbed her phone, and somewhere in between the Home screen and the browser, she found herself scrolling through photos. First, it was the pictures of Hari's bunnies, then the bunny buns with ZhanZhan, because Hari had been unable to get YingYing to sit still for the picture. And finally, there were the truly horrendous cupcakes they had made. They looked even worse than Darcie remembered. But something warm trickled through her veins at the reminder. She had enjoyed herself. She had laughed. She had smiled. Hari had made baking . . . fun?

It was the logical next step, although a stupid one, to go to Hari's social media accounts and start scrolling. Darcie already knew what she'd find; she knew Hari had been seeing Lily. A thought that had hurt at first but now Darcie just saw as a forgone conclusion. Lily was more Hari's speed.

But instead of beautifully lit photos of Lily's finest pastries, there was simply a photo of YingYing and Zhan-Zhan in soft focus with the words "what next?" over top of it. It had . . . a lot of comments. Too many comments. Darcie had never had so many comments on any of her posts in her life. She clicked it, because she was a glutton for punishment, and was greeted with a wall of text.

It was a rambling explanation about the end of Hari's partnership with Stargazer's that quoted "artistic differences" for the split but did not delve any further into why Hari might have parted ways with Lily. Darcie could hear the words in Hari's voice, as if ze was right there next to her, explaining. And before she had even finished, a smile tugged at the corners of her lips. She had missed Hari. She had not realized how much until that very moment.

Her fingers itched to reach out. To do what she hadn't done the entire time they had been friends: to call. But she stopped her thumbs just as they hovered over the little Call button on Hari's contact. Maybe it would be better if she texted instead. Darcie always felt like phone calls were so intrusive, but a text was something that could be ignored until there was time to respond to it, or not at all. On the other hand, texts were so impersonal. Would a texted apology be enough for the weeks of silence that had stretched between them? She wasn't sure.

In the end, it was a matter of cowardice. Darcie couldn't talk to Hari, not now, not yet. Not until she knew that Hari wasn't going to . . . well, maybe not yell at her, because Hari didn't seem the type to yell at anyone. But be stern with her. She'd just have to text.

The question was, what should she say?

I'm sorry.

No, she should wade into it. She shouldn't just start with that.

Hi, Hari. I just wanted to . . .

To what? *Check in? See how you were? Explain that I'm an emotionally constipated human being that doesn't know how to hold relationships because she's spent all of her life with flour and eggs?* No.

How are you?

Nope. That . . . just no.

I saw your post.

Yes, tell Hari that she was stalking zir. Good start. Hari would definitely want to be friends again after that. Darcie let out a breath, dropping the phone onto her desk with a soft clatter. Why was this so hard? Why couldn't she just be normal and say what she meant? What did she mean? Other than that she had messed up, big and she was deeply sorry for it, she didn't know. She . . . Why was apologizing so hard? Probably because she'd let it go for too long. If she'd just apologized right after the fight, maybe they could have moved past it with minimal talking. But now . . . now it was a Thing.

Dacie let out a breath. She'd just have to bite the bullet and do it. There was no way around it. Even if 'I'm sorry' seemed trite, it was the best way to open the conversation. The best way to start making things up to Hari.

Darcie: I'm sorry.

She sat her phone down again, half hoping that Hari wasn't still awake and that maybe they could have this conversation in the morning when she'd had a night to toss and turn over the stupidity of that one line. Maybe she could delete it? Could she unsend texts? She definitely should have said something else. She should delete it before Hari could . . .

The little Read notification had appeared under the text. Well. Damn. Darcie leaned forward, smashing her face against the cold pressboard desk. She had two options. She could send a follow-up text explaining, or she could wait for Hari to respond. Both sounded like torture. Maybe she'd just suffocate herself on the hard surface of her desk instead. Yeah, that sounded like a good—

Her phone began to vibrate. Not the short, clipped

vibration of a text but the long drawn-out one of a call. She jerked her head up and looked down at her phone, which had lit up again to show that Hari was calling. So much for options A and B; Hari had, of course, chosen option Y.

For a moment, a brief shining moment, she thought to ignore it. To pretend she was asleep. It was late enough, well past her bedtime. But then there was the pesky matter of time stamps and that Hari had called right away, so ze had clearly known when the text had come in. There was no letting it go to voicemail.

Still, her fingers trembled as she hit the green button and lifted the phone to her ear.

"Hi, Darcie!" Hari chirped, zir voice too bright in Darcie's ear.

Darcie opened her mouth to explain, to apologize, to say everything she was sorry for, or at the very least to respond. But her tongue seemed to have gone dry and useless in her mouth. She couldn't get a word past it.

"Darcie?" Hari asked when the silence stretched on for too long. "Are you all right? I know it's a little late for you, but you texted. So I figured you were up, and it was fine if I called. But if you were just about to go to bed or something, we can talk about this tomor—"

"Please forgive me." Darcie pressed the words past her lips, forcing them into the phone. It felt like ripping them from somewhere deep in her chest, but she couldn't let Hari go on. She couldn't let zir think that it had been a mistake, or a one-off, or whatever Hari's mind could work up, Darcie had no idea. "I overreacted, and I should have let you explain. And then I should have apologized sooner. I'm sorry."

"Oh uh . . . It's all right."

"No. It's not."

"Okay, well, maybe it's not. But I do forgive you." Hari's voice had gone up a little, like ze was smiling. That was a good sign, right?

"You do?" It couldn't be that easy. It just couldn't. And if it could, it shouldn't. Darcie had been . . . She had been rather nasty, and then she had flat-out ghosted Hari for a month. She didn't deserve that kind of kindness.

"Yup."

"Why?" Because she had to know. Darcie couldn't just accept that they could move past it with a lame 'I'm sorry,' and nothing more. There had to be . . . There was always more to it.

"People make mistakes," Hari said, and Darcie was sure if ze were standing before her, ze would be shrugging. "You were upset, and you have absolutely every right to be. Not at me, I didn't do anything wrong," Hari rushed to clarify. "But in general."

"That doesn't mean I should have taken it out on you."

"No. You shouldn't have. But what's done is done, and you apologized. So, the way I see it, I can either hold onto my upset and let it ruin what could potentially be a pretty awesome friendship, or I can let it go."

"Thank you."

"Don't thank me." Hari laughed. "Honestly, my forgiveness has nothing at all to do with you, Darcie. I'm forgiving you for myself. Purely selfish reasons here."

"Oh . . . uh . . . Okay."

"Also, that's not really why I called you."

"It's not?"

"Gosh, you're so cute," Hari mumbled almost to zirself, and Darcie could imagine zir shaking zir head. "No, it's not. I called because . . . Well . . . Because I want to help with the bakery. And before you say anything, I know Gyeong's isn't doing well. Don't ask me how I know, I just know. And I know you want to bring it back on your own. Trust me, I get it. But I've got some really good ideas and I'd really just love to stick it to—"

"Okay."

"Wait. What?"

"Please, help me." Darcie let the words rush out of her on a breath. As if she hadn't known she was going to say them before she had. But that wasn't true, was it? She'd known. She'd known she was going to ask for Hari's help. Because Hari . . . Hari would be able to do something she couldn't. "I need . . . I need help making Gyeong's . . ."

Darcie couldn't find the right words. More fun? More alive? More hip? More modern? More . . . something. It needed to be more something. She just didn't know what the more was. Maybe because she was still trying to process that she was asking someone to help her change her family's bakery, and it was hard to . . . get used to that thought.

"Making Gyeong's your own," Hari said, as if it were the easiest thing in the world. And maybe it was for zir. "All right. I've got some ideas. I'll come by tomorrow. I don't think any of these will require a lot of money, just some time and thought."

"I don't want to . . . " She pursed her lips around the words, trying to think of how to say what she meant to say. When had talking become so hard?

"Relax, Darcie, we'll keep the spirit of Gyeong's intact. Just because we make it yours doesn't mean it's any less your mother's or your grandfather's."

Darcie slumped back into her seat, letting Hari's words relax her entirely. That, not that she'd realized it until that very moment, had been exactly what she'd needed to hear. What she'd been needing to hear since she was eighteen and taking over after eomma's burial. What no one had ever said to her.

"I'll see you tomorrow, all right?"

"All right." Darcie nodded. "Thank you."

"That's your last one," Hari said with a soft laugh.

"What?"

"No more thank yous or sorries, all right? We're friends. This is what friends do for each other." Hari cleared zir throat as if ze had wanted to say more but had to swallow the words back. "Anyway, see you tomorrow!"

Then ze hung up and left Darcie staring at her phone. Darcie needed to . . . She'd need to . . . No. She'd worry about all of it tomorrow, when Hari got there. Ze would help. Ze had promised. She could worry about the menu and the bakery then. For now . . . For now, she needed to go home and rest.

EIGHTEEN

"She apologized," Hari said for what felt like the twentieth time as ze loaded up zir messenger bag with zir camera, tablet, sketchpad, paint swatches, anything and everything ze could imagine they'd need to get things started.

"Yes, I heard you. The first ten times." Katsuko sounded annoyed, her voice crackling with static over the phone. She was probably still in bed, tucked away under the covers in her tiny apartment. Hari had offered her zir guest room, but Katsuko wanted to do things on her own. Even if that meant living in what could arguably be termed a closet.

Hari didn't respond—ze didn't have to, and ze knew that. Katsuko would get to whatever point she was making, and till then, Hari would just focus on all the things ze could possibly need to talk about a revamp. A relaunch? Hari shrugged. Whatever Darcie wanted to call it, ze would be there.

"I just don't want you to get hurt. Not again."

"We're just friends. Nothing is going on. I'm just helping her get Gyeong's back on its feet."

Atsuko sighed. She'd heard that argument before, Hari knew she had. It was Hari's habit to help people, even if it was at the expense of zirself in some ways. There was a sound like Katsuko flopping back in bed on the other side of the line. "All right. Have fun storming the castle."

"You think it'll work?" Hari laughed, feeling lighter.

"Not a chance. Bye bye." And then Katsuko hung up without another word. Rude. Hari laughed, shaking zir head and slinging zir bag over zir shoulder.

Ze yawned into the back of zir hand, zoning out on the subway ride over to Darcie's. Hari hadn't slept much at all after their conversation. Too excited to get to work helping Darcie make Gyeong's her own. Which was normal, perfectly normal. Hari always got like that before a new project.

Darcie was sitting at the front table when ze got there. The one Hari had moved toward the window because the lighting was better. She had a printout in front of her and dark circles under her eyes, and the toe of her sensible work shoes was tapping against the tile floor.

Hari should have started their conversation with a good morning, a hello, a how are you, like a normal person. Like someone who knew how to have conversations with friends. But ze didn't. Instead, zir mouth said, "We don't have to change anything you don't want to. This is completely up to you, I'm only here to provide ideas and help execute what you like. Gyeong's is yours and will stay that way."

Darcie nodded her understanding, her hands folded neatly on the table in front of her. She looked . . . not excited. That wasn't good. Hari hoped ze wasn't pushing her into this. Ze hoped that she didn't feel like she didn't have a choice, but the reality was, she didn't. She needed to do something, or Lily would succeed in driving Gyeong's out of business.

"We'll do what we can without outside help, but if we do need it, I have people for that."

"You have people?"

"Yeah."

"Are you aware," Darcie said, pressing her mouth into a firm line to hide what seemed to be a smile, "that that makes you sound like a mob boss?"

"Who says I'm not?" Hari met her eyes, swallowing down a startled giggle at the sheer joy ze could see lining Darcie's eyes. They were crinkled, far more than Hari thought ze had ever seen them. Darcie was happy. Darcie was . . . They could make this work. They could save Gyeong's. Hari cleared zir throat, hoping to hide the blush that had begun to burn at the back of zir neck, and pulled out zir tablet. "I have some pictures of interiors I think you might like. Like I said, we'll do as much or as little as you want."

Darcie nodded, the smile falling from her face.

"Are you ready?"

"I think so," Darcie said, and she picked up her chair to scoot around the table.

And that's how it started, with Darcie's shoulder pressed into Hari's as they leaned over the tablet. Her soft voice telling Hari what she did or did not like about some of Hari's ideas, and them making a plan. A plan to paint, to take down the old menu, to put new bulbs in the glass cases, to get a logo made for the front window, to turn the bakery that had been Darcie's eomma's into Darcie's.

TWO WEEKS LATER, they had the bakery closed so that they could slap a fresh coat of paint and lacquer on everything in sight. Darcie had been particularly resistant to changing the color of the tables and chairs, which her appa had made himself. Hari didn't push it. Ze had made a deal; it was as much change as Darcie wanted and not a bit more. But they did need to be sanded down and refinished if nothing else.

They had recruited Darcie's employees, and Hari had blackmailed some of zir friends to help. Most of them had seemed more than happy to give up their weekend in the name of rehabbing Gyeong's. Hari hoped Darcie realized what a good sign that was, but it was always hard to tell with her. For her part, Darcie had been locked in the kitchen since dawn.

"I can't believe you gave her homework," Aura muttered, shaking her head.

Hari wasn't exactly sure why Aura was there; she had said she didn't want to help. In fact, she'd specifically complained that she had other, more important plans that weekend than sitting around in the matching mechanic jumpers Hari had gotten them. Hari refused to tell anyone where from. Ze had also refused to tell anyone how ze had gotten them embroidered so quickly. It paid to know people . . . or to know a witch, more specifically. And Gwydion owed Darcie at least that much for what they'd done. Besides, Gwydion had agreed they'd make for super cute pictures for the website and the official grand re-opening shots Hari planned to take.

"Who gives their girlfriend homework?" Eero nodded his agreement from where he sat with a can of poly between his legs. Well, that was probably why Aura was there. Honestly, if they would just get on with asking each other out, then they could stop this will-they-won't-they nonsense they were doing. And Hari's life could go back to being unbearably boring and drama free. Which . . . ze thought ze might like at this point.

"She's not my girlfriend," Hari said, for what might have been the tenth time since they had started working that morning. Every time ze said it, the others seemed to believe it a little less. The late nights spent pouring over pictures and plans and financials probably wasn't helping. But that didn't make it any less true. Darcie was a friend. A good friend. And Hari just wanted her to be happy. That was all.

"Okay well your not-girlfriend is crying in the back." Katsuko peeked around the display case she was working on.

"What?" Hari jerked to zir feet, nearly knocking over the chair ze had been working on. "What do you mean she's crying?"

"Just what I said, she's crying." Katsuko shifted in her seat, presumably to get a better look. "You want me to—?"

"No!" Hari scrambled across the front of the bakery to get to the swinging doors. "I do not want you to do anything."

"Suit yourself." Katsuko shrugged and went back to working on the display case.

Hari nodded to zirself, carefully schooling zir features and heading back into the kitchen. Darcie was there, her shoulders hunched over the menu Hari had asked her to go over. They both knew Gyeong's couldn't survive offering the wide range of things it did all the time. Something would have to give, whether Darcie liked it or not. Still, Hari had known it would be difficult for her and had wanted to give her all the time she needed. Hence the homework.

"Darcie . . . " Hari said softly, moving to stand beside her but carefully keeping zir distance. "Is everything all right?"

Darcie released a choked, wet sound, but it sounded more like a laugh than a sob. When she lifted her head, her eyes were glassy, but she was smiling. A sad, broken, hurting thing. "I should have known."

"What? You should have known what? What's going on?" Hari stepped in closer, pressing zir shoulder into Darcie's side as best as ze could. It wasn't a hug, but it was the best ze could hope for right now when they were . . . whatever they were.

Darcie didn't answer, she just let her phone smack against the steel table loud enough that it made Hari wince. She gestured vaguely to the still lit screen, and Hari looked down at the article. Interview, actually. With Lily. Claiming that Gyeong's was selling . . . That Darcie had . . . Hari felt zirself shaking. Ze wasn't sure when ze had started, but ze was now, rage making Hari unsteady.

"I told her I wasn't going to expose her. Why would she do this?" Hari didn't need an answer, it was clear. Lily wanted to strike while Darcie was at her most vulnerable, kick her while she was down. There was no better way to ensure that Gyeong's stayed closed than to break Darcie's spirit. And there was no better way to do that than to tell everyone in New York how Gyeong's was built on lies. How Darcie had stolen her recipes from Lily, not the other way around. How Darcie was a liar, a cheat. And the public would believe Lily too, because she was pretty and soft, and because she'd put herself out there since opening her bakery, whereas Darcie never had. And it wasn't about the truth; it was about public perception, about how things looked.

"We should just . . . " Darcie breathed out, her hands

clutching at the menu. She'd actually managed to mark a couple of the items on the list as specials or seasonal. It was a good start. "We should just quit."

"Do you want to quit?" Hari asked, pressing the button on the side of the phone to lock it and hide the article away. "Is that what you want?"

"You've already put so much work into this . . . " Darcie wasn't meeting Hari's eyes. She was looking down at the menu, watching her fingers trace a line of letters.

"That's not what I asked, Darcie. This isn't about me. This isn't about the bakery. This is about you. Do you want to give up? Are you ready to move on to something else? Whatever you want, I'll help. But it's your choice."

"But eomma—"

"Your mom would want you to be happy. So would your grandpa. Everyone would want you to be happy. I want you to be happy. If this doesn't make you happy anymore, we walk away." Hari tried not to pay attention to the word we and how it had slipped from zir tongue like it meant something. It didn't.

"And if I don't want to walk away?" Darcie looked up finally, her eyes set in a look of sudden determination. It was . . . It was *beautiful*. It made Hari's breath catch in her chest.

"Then we've got work to do." Hari smiled tightly.

"What do you need me to do?"

"Exactly what you've been doing. Cut this menu down, then you and Heather can work on turning everything that's left into something more visually appealing." Hari tapped zir finger against the paper. It would be better to keep Darcie focused on this. To keep her out of the messy social media drama that was about to ensue. "Relaunch is the beginning of next month, this needs to be done by then."

"And what are you going to do?"

"Take care of *this*. Call in a few favors." Hari said, tapping zir fingers right beside the hibernating phone. "Don't you worry your pretty little head about it; I've got it. Now, show me what you were thinking for the new menu, yeah?"

Darcie nodded, her shoulders relaxing as she put her attention back on the thing she could control, the thing she was good at: baking. Hari would handle the rest.

NINETEEN

Darcie had thought it would hurt, cutting down Gyeong's old menu. That it would feel like cutting off a limb. It had been built before she was born and remained unchanged all through her life. It was like it was a piece of eomma. Only, that wasn't right, she was realizing. Everything she had clung to after she'd lost eomma had been—Well, not wrong but mistaken. She had treated Gyeong's as a security blanket, she realized, standing and looking out at the refinished dining area. But that time was past now.

When Hari had given her this assignment ze had held her hands and smiled at her, and said, "*You're* your eomma's legacy."

It had made Darcie feel oddly lighter. Made her feel like she could do this, she could do what she needed to do. She was allowed to make Gyeong's hers. So, she threw herself into cutting down the menu. Only keeping the recipes she loved the most, or the best sellers. Everything else became a rotating special or something they only sold seasonally. It was better that way, she realized. It meant she'd have more time at the end of the day to do other things. She could finally have a life outside of the bakery.

"I think I should warn you," Heather said, the bell over the door announcing her arrival, "I'm not super artistic. I mostly just know how to follow a recipe. I'm a chem major."

"That's fair." Darcie bit back a smile and turned back into the kitchen where she had everything set up to make their test batches. They needed to take the recipes that were left and "rebrand" them as Hari had said. Turn them into something worthy of being splashed across social media. "Hari sent over some ideas."

"Yeah, ze sent them to me too. I guess ze thought maybe they'd spark something. But I don't . . . I don't sit there and look at food online all the time." Heather shrugged, looking sheepish. Darcie wondered, not for the first time, why Heather had even taken up the job at the bakery. It didn't really seem to make sense. But she was a decent baker and, Darcie was beginning to realize, a good friend.

"Well, we've got the weekend. And Hari said if we needed to, we could call zir." Darcie pulled the dough she'd made the day before from the rising rack and flopped it onto the steel table.

"Yeah, I'll bet ze did." Heather said it like she didn't mean for Darcie to hear. So Darcie gave her the credit of pretending she hadn't.

"I think we definitely need to do the bunny buns." The dough was sticky between her fingers as she ripped off a chunk. Slapping it onto the little scale, she let out a satisfied hum. "But do you think we should do any other animals?"

"Other than that fish bread—"

"Bungeo-ppang, it means carp bread."

"Right, that." Heather nodded. "Other than the bungeo-ppang, I think we don't need a ton of animals. We just need to find ways to make the other recipes more visually appealing, right?"

Darcie hummed thoughtfully. "The soborro, instead of filling them before we cook them, maybe we could cut them and make them into a sandwich cookie?"

"That's that streusel thing, right?"

Darcie nodded.

"Could we color the cream maybe? Not too bright, but just a couple of drops to make them a pretty pastel?"

"We may have to adjust it to keep it from being too wet, but I don't see why not." Darcie's hands worked fast, forming a neat row of bunnies on the pan sat in the middle of the table.

"There are a few of the others I think we could use a mold for." Heather's fingers were tapping softly in front of her. She hadn't reached out to help make the buns, but Darcie found she didn't care. There was something restful about the repetitive motions of twisting dough balls and cutting little bunny ears into them. Something . . . at peace about doing this while talking to someone who she had gradually realized was a friend.

"If we do, I want the molds custom made. I don't want anything off the internet." Darcie wrinkled her nose in thought, moving the tray to the oven.

"And we'll have to keep them labeled, so the same mold is always used for the same pastry." Heather pulled out her phone to type up a list as they talked, her lips twisting into a smile. "That should be easy enough though."

"It should." Darcie moved on to the dough for the kkwabaegi. "Any cute pancake ideas for the chalbori-ppang?"

"Those have a filling, right?"

"Mhm."

"Shape them like little bears with faces?"

"I thought we said we didn't want to do a bunch of animals?"

Heather shrugged, laughing a little. "Sorry."

"No, it's all right, it's a good thought." The fryer popped angrily behind her, the sound of it adding to the gentle hum of the kitchen.

"As for the molds, does the Gyeong family have any like . . . traditional ones? From when you guys lived in Korea?"

"Hmm . . . not sure. I'll have to do some digging. Maybe reach out to some of the family who still lives there. That's a good idea though, thank you, Heather. You've been a big help."

"No problem! That's what friends are for!" Heather tilted her head, long dark hair falling over her shoulder, and Darcie felt herself smile. Friends. They were friends. Darcie had friends. "I'll email you this list when we're done, so you have record of it."

Darcie nodded, ducking her smile back down as she went back to twisting the donuts.

HEATHER HAD LEFT for the day—she had a paper she needed to write for the following week, and Darcie didn't want her grades to slip just because she was helping out at Gyeong's. After she'd left, Darcie had called Hari and put zir on speaker just to fill the silence of the empty kitchen.

"I'm going to have Yuuki make you one of his epic cooking playlists," Hari said, zir voice tinny but warm as it bounced off the metal of the kitchen.

"I like instrumental music."

Hari snorted, but it sounded fond. "Of course you do.

Well, fine, I'll look at some lo-fi jams for you. I guess we can't all belt out Adele while we work."

"I don't even know who Adele is." Darcie pursed her lips to keep Hari from hearing the smile in the words.

"Liar." Hari laughed. "I have seen your phone."

"I don't know what you're talking about."

Hari let out a soft chuckle, and Darcie could imagine zir shaking zir head. It was a good image. A fond image. It made Darcie's insides warm in a strange, delightful way. She liked it, she decided.

"Heather said something earlier," Darcie said, her fingers sticky with sugar. "She mentioned looking into the Gyeong history to see if my family used any traditional molds. Could you send me the information for that blogger who specializes in historical places again? I'm afraid I may have . . . deleted it."

"Yeah, sure. I think you'll like them, they're pretty cool. Super serious, like you."

"I'm not serious," Darcie huffed. But she was grateful that Hari had pushed past what could have been an awkward discussion about when they had been fighting. About how Darcie had made things difficult for a time. About how she had deleted every message or e-mail from Hari in stupidly blind anger. A weakness. It was nice to not have someone call her out on it.

"Sure you're not. You're like . . . the least serious person in all of Manhattan."

Darcie huffed again, but she felt laughter clinging to the edges of her tongue like syrup.

"You're laughing, I can hear it," Hari said, amazement coating zir tinny voice.

"Well, you are very funny."

"Liar," Hari laughed, zir voice going soft around the

edges. Hari yawned into the phone. "Sorry. It was . . . It's been a long week."

"You should go to sleep. You've worked very hard." Darcie hummed softly. "I—" She stopped, took a breath, and forced herself not to swallow the words down. "I appreciate all you've done for me. This is—" Another deep breath. "It's a lot."

"Hey, what did I say?"

"That was not a thank you."

"It technically was."

Darcie stared at the phone, unblinking.

"You're doing that thing, aren't you? The annoyed staring thing. Next time, we really need to video chat so I can see you do it." Hari snickered. "I mean, if you're going to be petty with me, I'd like to see your cute face when you do it."

Darcie did not blush. Her ears just got hot. Which meant . . . absolutely nothing. "You need to rest. We have a long few days ahead of us. Relaunch in two weeks."

"Relaunch in two weeks," Hari agreed. "All right, I'm off. Try not to stay up too late." Hari yawned again. "Give that big, beautiful brain of yours a rest, okay?"

"Okay."

"Good night."

"Sweet dreams." Darcie waited until Hari hung up and then she slumped forward against the table, nearly putting the entire front of her apron into the ball of dough she'd been kneading. Her phone buzzed, and she pulled away to smile down at a text from Hari.

Hari: Listen to this so you don't get lonely.

There was a link below to a playlist, which Darcie

promptly turned on, then smiled a little at the music filling up the space around her.

Hari: ZhanZhan and YingYing say good night!
   / (=⌒x⌒=) \ / (=˙·˙=) \
Darcie: Hari, rest.
Hari: right right I'm going
(^3^)-☆Chu!!

Darcie chuckled, shaking her head.

"Ze likes you."

Darcie yelped, clutching her chest and lifting her eyes to glare at Gwydion. They had perched themselves on the corner of the worktable, legs crossed and dangling, as they ripped off a piece of still-warm kkwabaegi to pop into their mouth. Once she'd gotten over the shock, she frowned at Gwydion.

"What?" Darcie asked, trying not to sound defensive. She didn't need to be defensive. Nothing was going on. Hari was just . . . Hari was just the nicest person Darcie had ever known. Sweet and kind and willing to do anything for another person. Hari was just *amazing*.

"These are good. Like *really* good." Gwydion murmured happily around a mouthful of dough. Then their perfectly lined eyes narrowed on Darcie. "You're happy."

"It would seem so." Darcie turned back to where she'd been kneading dough for the following day's test loaves. It looked . . . Damn. It was over kneaded. She wondered if she could salvage it or if she'd destroyed all the air that had been inside.

Gwydion slid from the table, their heels clacking against the tile as they made their way over to lean into Darcie's line of sight. They would not be ignored. "I could lift the curse now."

"You could?" Darcie lifted her head, blinking in confusion. She hadn't thought . . . She'd thought it had to be broken. But then, if it had to be broken, why were her bakes still determined by her mood when she'd finally found happiness again? When she'd finally learned how to move past the grief that seemed to have kept her stuck for so many years. Why hadn't her bakes gone back to normal?

Gwydion nodded. "You've learned to let go and found your love of this place again. There's no reason to leave it."

Darcie couldn't help the way her heart sped in her chest. She could be free. Free to have a crappy baking day that didn't affect her product. Free to go back to how things were. To wallowing. To being lonely. To . . . no. She didn't want that. She couldn't go back. Not really. "There also isn't any reason for you to lift it."

Gwydion's lips twitched into a little smile, their red braid cascading dangerously close to the ruined milk bread dough as they tilted their head. "No?"

Darcie took a breath, then let it out and forced with it the words she'd been holding close to her chest since Hari had told her they would remake Gyeong's into her own. Since Hari had looked her in the eyes and told her that *she* was her eomma's legacy, not this bakery. Since this whole project had started. "Baking makes me happy. And my happy bakes are so good, they make other people happy. I don't want to give that up."

"There will be bad days," Gwydion argued, but their golden eyes were crinkly at the edges.

"There are always bad days."

"There are."

"But I'm not alone anymore."

Gwydion smiled, eyes turning into crescents as they stepped back from Darcie, their hands on their hips. "Well, would you look at that? I didn't even have to make you move in with me!"

"What?"

"Nothing." Gwydion flicked their wrist as if shaking away a bit of dust. "Well, I wish you all the best on relaunch day."

"Will you be there?" Darcie wasn't sure why she wanted to know. Was she scared that Gwydion would show up and make a mess of things? Or did she want the witch there to prove to them that she'd changed, that she'd learned, to see her triumph?

"Wouldn't miss it for the world." Gwydion winked. "Tell your new beau I love the jump suits ze had made. I hope you guys wear them on opening day, they're super cute!"

And then they disappeared, leaving a spray of glitter that Darcie could only hope was nontoxic and didn't get in any of the dough. She already had to remake the milk bread.

TWENTY

In the end, it wasn't nearly as hard to make Lily back down as Hari had thought it would be. Ze had thought that there would be an all-out social media war. Hari was prepared for it, although ze had never really participated in one before. But ze couldn't take a passive role, not when Lily was slandering Darcie as she was. Not when it seemed that this was some kind of weird revenge-of-the-ex game to her. But it wasn't.

"If it means that much to you," Lily said, shrugging as if she hadn't caused Darcie to have a panic attack in the middle of her own kitchen, an action that made Hari quietly furious, "I'll withdrawal my claim."

"The damage is already done, and you know it." Hari's hands tightened into fists where ze had stuffed them into zir pockets.

"Maybe, but she's got you helping her. I'm sure between the two of you, there's a way to combat the bad press, right?" Lily leaned forward, her elbows pressed into her desk. Hari was grateful they were having this argue—*discussion* in Lily's office. Ze didn't want to be seen shouting at a rival baker in the middle of her bakery. It wouldn't look good for Darcie. There was a smile on Lily's face that Hari had long since decided ze didn't like.

"The blog article with the history of Gyeong's goes out soon. It'll have all the proof we need that you lied."

Lily leaned back in her chair, her posture relaxed and insolent as she folded her hands across her stomach. "That's fine."

Hari's eyes narrowed. Lily was too relaxed about this, much too relaxed. This could ruin her. If it got out that she had been stealing recipes for years. If people knew that nothing she made was really her own. "You seem awfully . . . nonchalant about this."

"Competition is good for business," Lily said, unbothered by the scathing look that Hari was giving her. "Strife is good for business."

"What?"

Lily laughed a little, shaking her head. "K-town is big enough for the both of us, Hari. We don't need to push each other out of the neighborhood just to survive. But if people think we're trying, if it looks like we're fighting to one up each other the whole time . . . then they'll want to see what all the fuss is about, won't they? They'll come to Stargazer's to see what we have, then go to Gyeong's to see what they have. They'll compare and contrast us. Even if they don't choose sides, we'll become the dueling bakeries. It'll be good press."

"That's what this was all about? Good press?" Hari wasn't sure when ze had started shaking with the poorly suppressed rage, but ze had. The realization that it had been a manipulation, all of it, from the very beginning, set something off in zir that Hari was sure ze would never be able to smother again. How could Lily be so . . . blasé about this?

Like it was just a game, not someone's livelihood she'd almost ruined?

"Maybe not at first. But after a fashion? Yes. Well, and I didn't really want to see Gyeong's go under. At the rate Darcie was going, it was inevitable. So I lit a fire under her, didn't I?"

"This isn't . . . It's not an anime or some twisted K-drama!" Hari let out a shaky laugh, rolling zir eyes. Lily lifted one shoulder in a half shrug.

"It really kind of is."

"You are either the best or the worst friend I've ever met."

Lily's expression shifted, her smile turning sadder around the edges. "Do me a favor?"

"What?"

"Don't tell Darcie about this little chat. Just let her go on being furious at me for this. It'll be good for both of us."

"You don't want her to know that you were trying to help her? Admittedly, in the most messed up way possible." Hari felt everything unclench, zir eyes widening. If Lily had done all of this to help Darcie as she claimed, Hari was sure she'd want to be friends again. Wouldn't she?

Lily let out a breath, and suddenly she looked much younger, like a little girl who had lost her best friend and didn't know how to make things better. And older all at the same time. "No. I think it's better we keep up this whole 'enemies' thing. Good press, like I said."

"Maybe if you apologized to her . . . "

Lily shook her head.

"What happened between you two?"

"We weren't good for each other. Not all people are. Not all *friends* are." That didn't change the way Lily felt about Darcie. She didn't say it, but Hari could see it in the way her eyes fell to her desk. Lily loved Darcie as all friends do. But there had been something, something that had broken between them. Something that had made her realize that whatever they were to each other, it wasn't good.

"You should try apologizing. People change. Maybe it's different now."

"Good luck on the relaunch. I'll be rooting for you two. Fighting," Lily said instead of answering. "Now, if you'll excuse me, I have a bakery to run."

Lily rose and ushered Hari to the door. Hari stopped, zir hand resting on the doorframe to keep Lily from shoving zir out if it came to that. Not that ze thought she would. She didn't seem the type.

"What is it?" Lily asked, crossing her arms over her chest.

"Just think about what I said, all right? You've both changed, and a little apology can go a long way." Hari dropped zir hands from the doorframe and headed back out into the kitchen, followed closely by Lily. "And she could use friends. So just . . . think about it?"

"If I promise to think about it, will you let me get back to work?" Lily rolled her eyes.

Hari nodded, pleased with zirself.

"Fine, I'll think about it."

THE DAY ROSE TOO bright and too early, and Hari hadn't slept nearly enough the night before. But that didn't matter, none of it mattered, because it was relaunch day, and Hari was going to be there to see Darcie thrive.

"You don't look like you slept," Darcie said in that way of

hers which could often be misconstrued as rude but that Hari had learned meant she was actually worried.

"Who needs sleep when you've got caffeine?" Hari grinned, bumping zir shoulder into Darcie's and politely not mentioning the dark circles lining her own eyes. Because ze was nice like that. A smile split Hari's face as Darcie took the offered tea and sipped carefully.

"How much longer?"

"Half an hour. But there was a line down the block when I got here already, so we'll be busy." Hari crossed one leg over the other where ze was leaning against the counter, the pale blue jumpsuit wrinkling at the knees. "You sure you don't want me to run the register?"

Darcie shook her head. "Sarah and Heather are here for that. I need you up front taking pictures for the website and the blog posts."

"Aye aye, captain!" Hari did a little mini salute and couldn't help but delight in the tiny smile it pulled from Darcie.

"After this—" Darcie started and then stopped herself, taking an unnecessarily large gulp of tea that had to burn all the way down, if the grimace on her face was anything to go by.

"Yes?" Hari prompted, pressing zir shoulder more firmly into Darcie's. A reminder and a comfort all in one. Or at least Hari hoped that's what it was. Ze wanted Darcie to know that ze was there for her and that ze would never judge her. Ze also wanted Darcie to finish that sentence, like . . . yesterday.

Darcie pursed her lips, her eyes drifting to a spot over Hari's shoulder instead of making eye contact.

"Yeeeeees?" Hari pushed, taking in the slight blush that had settled into Darcie's earlobes.

Darcie huffed out an annoyed breath, squeezed her eyes shut, and when she opened them again, she met Hari's gaze head-on. "I think I'd like to take you out after this. Dinner. Someplace nice."

"Not as a thank you, right?" Hari swallowed down the rabid joy that threatened to turn zir voice into a wobbling, giggling mess. "It's a date, right?"

Darcie nodded once, firmly. She was making eye contact, but her gaze was jerking around Hari's face as if looking for some sign that ze would say no.

Hari moved onto zir toes and pressed a kiss to Darcie's cheek. "I'd like that very much."

Darcie let out a long gasp of a breath, a smile crinkling her eyes at the corners. "Okay. Good. You ready for the rush?"

Hari threw back what was left of zir coffee, hissing around the faint ache of it still being almost too hot, and stood from the counter. "Let's do this."

The doors opened, and the line that had formed outside streamed into the bakery, and from there, Hari lost zirself to the constant hum of customers. At some point, it got to be too much even for seasoned bakery assistants like Heather and Sarah, and Hari had to step in and help fill orders and bus tables to keep people happy. But that was all right. There was a certain thrill to knowing that Gyeong's was so busy that it may need more staff.

At the end of the day, as the last of the customers wandered out and Heather turned the sign on the door, Hari's feet were throbbing. Ze dropped into a chair near the window and flopped back to let zir neck hang limp.

"Tired?" Darcie asked, her voice soft and playful.

"Hells yes. Why didn't you tell me that a busy day in the bakery was going to be so stressful?" Hari groaned, not even having the strength to pull zir head back up so ze could glare at Darcie, who was inevitably laughing at zir.

"Would you have helped if you'd known?"

"Ah! So you tricked me? I see how it is! Such deceitfulness. Dishonor. Dishonor on you. Dishonor on your cow. Dishonor!"

"My cow?"

Hari flicked zir wrist carelessly, still not bothering to pull zir head back up. The world looked rather silly upside down, and it was making zir a little dizzy. But it just sounded like so much work to sit up straight again.

"Is there anything left over for lil ol' me?" a new voice asked. Gwydion appeared a moment later, standing behind Hari so ze could watch them in that weird upside-down view of the world.

"I saved you a bunny bun." Darcie sounded like she was smiling. At the witch?! Hari lifted zir head finally to give Darcie an incredulous look.

"Nothing sweet?"

"Afraid not. You'll have to come early tomorrow if you want one of the sweet pastries. They went first." Darcie shrugged, content to sit and watch Gwydion huff and pout.

"How early?"

"Early enough." Darcie's lips twitched in silent laughter.

"Fine." Gwydion huffed and disappeared again.

"That was the witch," Hari said, eyes glued to the faint glimmer of glitter that was settling onto the floor.

"It was." Darcie sipped from her water bottle.

"The one who cursed you."

"Yes."

"Did we break the curse?" Hari leaned forward, pressing zir face in closer to Darcie's, an obnoxious smile splitting zir lips. "Was it true love's kiss?"

Darcie blinked at zir blandly, but there was amusement flickering in her eyes. *Cute. She was so cute.* "No. It was not."

"Then what was it? Magic bunny buns?"

"No. I am still cursed. Or . . . blessed, rather."

"What?" Hari's head cocked to one side, hair falling limply from zir messy bun.

"I have decided to keep Gwydion's blessing." Darcie set the bottle of water on the table between them and smiled at Hari. "To make the most of it."

Hari smiled brightly, and in the next moment, leaned across the table. "I'm going to kiss you now, okay?"

Darcie nodded quickly, and then Hari was pressing zir smile onto Darcie's lips.

TWENTY-ONE

In the pre-dawn quiet of New York, Darcie stood humming along to the playlist Hari had made her and putting the finishing touches on the day's bakes. It had been a few weeks since the successful re-launch and their first real date. No more than a couple of days since Hari had first called Darcie zir girlfriend. It all felt so new and so . . . right. Darcie had decided not to look too closely at it. Not yet.

Into the silences of not looking and the city just waking up, Darcie's phone buzzed. A moment later, a text notification from an unsaved number flashed across the screen. Darcie turned to wash her hands free of flour and dough, then grabbed up her phone to read the little preview on her Lock screen.

> Unknown Number: Darcie? I hope this is still your number.
>> Who am I kidding? Of course it is.
>> This is Lily. I just wanted to say . . .

Darcie opened the text app to watch as the little typing

bubbles appeared and disappeared over and over. Typing. Erasing. Typing. Erasing. Darcie wasn't sure what Lily was finding so hard to say, but she knew it would be best to let her say it. Interrupting her would just make her chicken out. That much hadn't changed about Lily.

In the meantime, Darcie went to add Lily to her contacts, unsure if this was going to become a regular thing or not. She figured it was better to know Lily's number than to not. In case of an emergency. A bakery emergency.

> Lily: I'm sorry for everything. I hope one day you can forgive me.

It was a little simple for Lily. Too straightforward. But that's how Darcie knew it was genuine. And for a moment, she considered just not responding. She remembered that she did not owe Lily anything, least of all her forgiveness. But then she remembered how eomma had once said that forgiving was not forgetting. And how Hari had said that zir forgiveness was for zir, not for the person asking for it. So she opened the message app and started typing.

> Darcie: I forgive you.

AND THAT WAS how the baker learned to let go of the past and find happiness in the present.

EPILOGUE

Darcie had never been much a fan of weddings. Not that she'd been to many, but they always seemed over the top and empty. Not this one. Not this one, where Yuuki and Alrik were already crying, even before Yuuki had walked down the aisle. Alrik looking every bit the Prince Charming in a white corseted waistcoat and rubbing at the corners of his eyes with his gloved hands as if he could hide his tears that way. She hadn't gotten the full story on them yet, but she'd gotten enough from Hari to know that Alrik had never thought he'd get to marry someone who he really loved.

Gwydion blew loudly into an embroidered handkerchief beside Alrik before they met Blaze's eyes and mouthed, "You're next."

Blaze rolled his eyes but didn't say anything to the contrary, which seemed to take every ounce of restraint he had. Instead, he leaned in to murmur to Fable, "Here comes Yuuki."

The music changed. Hari and Katsuko's steps were stilted, timed to the music in a way that only the truly dramatic could manage. They were wearing matching midnight blue suits. Hari winked at Darcie when ze passed, and Darcie could only roll her eyes fondly. Then came Yuuki, escorted by his parents.

Once Yuuki was deposited before Alrik, his parents took their seats, and Katsuko flopped down beside Darcie. The ceremony was short. Yuuki and Alrik had written their own vows, but instead of saying them, as Darcie thought was normal practice, they exchanged them like love letters and read them silently before tucking them away. Then there was more crying, and some I dos and kissing, and before Darcie fully understood that the actual marriage part of the wedding was over, Hari was before her, holding out a hand.

"Ready to get this party started?" ze asked.

"You're going to make me dance, aren't you?"

"Of course I am. That's why I told you to wear sensible shoes." Hari laughed, zir ringlets of deep purple hair falling over zir shoulder. Darcie looked down at her shoes. Loafers. Stylish, well-polished loafers that went perfectly with the closely tailored black velvet suit Hari had helped her find. But still, loafers.

"Is this how it's always going to be?" Darcie let Hari pull her to her feet, her eyes flicking back over to Yuuki and Alrik. Yuuki was dragging Alrik to the big table they'd set into the middle of the dining space for themselves and their nearest and dearest. Several smaller tables floated around it, already filling up with guests.

"Well, I can't promise we'll have a wedding every weekend. But yeah, I think I'm going to spend quite some time asking you to dance and laughing as you roll your eyes when you agree."

"Is that a proposal?"

"It's not not a proposal." Hari winked. "How'd I do?"

Darcie tilted her head as if considering, biting down on the inside of her cheek to hide her smile, and said, "It could use work."

Hari laughed, long and loud, zir head thrown back in zir joy. And then ze pulled Darcie in close. "Come on, dance with me before I'm too full of cake to bother."

"All right." She nodded and let Hari sweep her out onto the glittering dance floor for the first of many dances.

ACKNOWLEDGMENTS

First off, thank you—the reader—for reading Darcie and Hari's story. I hope you enjoyed their journey of self discovery, and maybe learned something about healing in the process.

Their story might be over, but this is not the last you have heard of Gwydion and their interesting curses. So, be on the look out for more from them.

Next, I'd like the think my small hoard of beta-readers. You guys gave some excellent insight, and I really appreciate the quick turn around that made this release possible!

And last but certainly not least, thank you to my small writing support group. Tiss, Elle, and Jasmine—without you there would be no Lou.

ABOUT THE AUTHOR

Born and raised in a small town near the Chesapeake Bay, Lou Wilham grew up on a steady diet of fiction, arts and crafts, and Old Bay. After years of absorbing everything, there was to absorb of fiction, fantasy, and sci-fi she was left with a serious creative habit that just won't quit. These days, she spends much of her time writing, drawing, and chasing a very short Basset Hound named Sherlock.

When not, daydreaming up new characters to write and draw she can be found crocheting, making cute bookmarks, and binge-watching whatever happens to catch her eye.

Learn more about Lou and her future projects on her website: http://louinprogress.net or join her mailing list at: http://subscribepage.com/mailermailer

MORE BOOKS YOU'LL LOVE

If you enjoyed this story, please consider leaving a review.

Then check out more books from Midnight Tide Publishing!

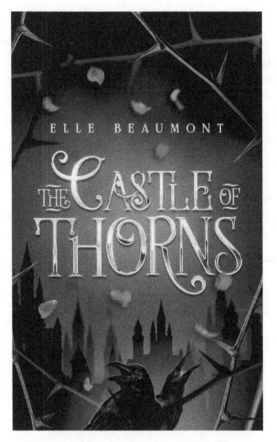

The Castle of Thorns by Elle Beaumont

To end the murders, she must live with the beast of the forest.

After surviving years with a debilitating illness that leaves her weak, Princess Gisela must prove that she is more than her ailment. She discovers her father, King Werner, has been growing desperate for the herbs that have been her survival. So much so, that he's willing to cross paths with a deadly legend of Todesfall Forest to retrieve her remedy.

Knorren is the demon of the forest, one who slaughters anyone who trespasses into his land. When King Werner steps into his territory, desperately pleading for the herbs that control his beloved daughter's illness, Knorren toys with the idea. However, not without a cost. King Werner must deliver his beloved Gisela to Knorren or suffer dire consequences.

With unrest spreading through the kingdom, and its people growing tired of a king who won't put an end to the demon of Todesfall Forest, Gisela must make a choice. To become Knorren's prisoner forever, or risk the lives of her beloved people.

For fans of Sarah J. Maas, Jennifer Armentrout, A.G. Howard, Casey L. Bond, and Naomi Novik.

Add to your TBR
Available Nov. 3 2021

Lyrics & Curses by Candace Robinson

Their love for music sparked a curse...

Lark Espinoza could get lost in her music—and she's not so sure anyone in her family would even care to find her. Her trendy, party-loving twin sister and her mother-come-lately Beth, who's suddenly sworn off men and onto homemaking, don't understand her love of cassette tapes, her loathing of the pop scene, or her standoffish personality. For outcast Lark, nothing feels as much like a real home as working at

Bubble's Oddities store and trying to attract the attention of the cute guy who works at the Vinyl shop next door—the same one she traded lyrical notes with in class.

Auden Ellis silences the incessant questions in his own head with a steady stream of beats. Despite the unconditional love of his aunt-turned-mother, he can't quit thinking about the loss of his parents—or the possibility he might end up afflicted with his father's issues. Despite his connection with lyric-loving Lark, Auden keeps her at arm's length because letting her in might mean giving her a peek into something dangerous.

When two strangers arrive in town, one carrying a mysterious, dark object and the other playing an eerie flute tune, Lark and Auden find that their painful pasts have enmeshed them in a cursed future. Now, they must come to terms with their budding attraction while helping each other challenge the reflection they see in the mirror. If they fail, they'll be trapped for eternity in a place beyond reality.

Perfect for fans of Stranger Things and Pretty in Pink. Set in 1985, Lyrics & Curses is full of nostalgia, romance, mystery, and a story like no other.

Add to your TBR
Available Now

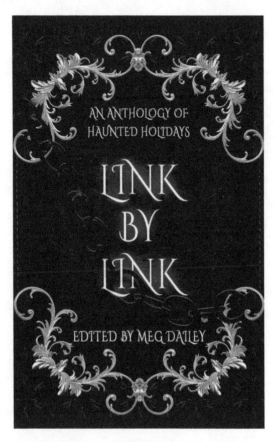

A Haunted Holidays Anthology

"'I wear the chain I forged in life,' replied the Ghost. 'I made it link by link...'"-Charles Dickens, A Christmas Carol

Link by Link is a collection of 9 stories of ghosts, spirits, and creatures unnamed, all come to teach lessons we won't soon forget. From sweet Christmas tales to terrifying holiday hauntings, these stories take a dive into the past in the hopes of creating a better—or at least different—future

Add to your TBR
Available Now

CREDITS

Cake Shape made by FreePik from
www.flaticon.com